ORCAS INTRIGUE

Book 1 of
The Chameleon Chronicles

Laura Gayle

BOOK VIEW CAFE

Book View Café Publishing Cooperative

Second Edition

ISBN: 978-1-61138-639-4

www.bookviewcafe.com
Book View Café Publishing Cooperative

For Bogdan and Carol Kulminski
With thanks for their hospitality and friendship

CHAPTER 1

When my latest relationship imploded on my twenty-seventh birthday, I did the only reasonable thing: I picked up and moved to a remote island in the Pacific Northwest.

It was a blur, really. One moment I was reeling from a breakup when I'd been expecting a proposal; and the next, it seemed, I was in line for the last ferry of the night, my car packed with everything it would hold, crying so steadily that I wasn't sure if it was rain or my tears that made the windshield look like that.

"Stupid, Cam, stupid," I chastised myself. I'd vanished again, just when Kevin had asked me to open my heart, to let him in. I'd tried, and when it had gone so sour, I'd panicked and vanished. I always vanished. I couldn't help it.

I closed my eyes and sniffled. "So now you're running away," I whispered in the dark. "Again." *No, I'm running toward*, I told myself.

Maybe if I said it enough times, I'd even believe it was true.

It could be true. The caretaking job held promise. And really, Orcas Island is not all that remote. It's the largest of the San Juan Islands, and there are ferries several times a day. You can get there from Seattle in a mere four hours...or five...or not until the next day, if you miss that last ferry.

Well, I wasn't missing it. "Now boarding, lanes three and four, with stops at Lopez, Shaw, and Orcas Island." Ahead of me, tail-lights flared as people started their engines. We crawled ahead, following the directions of the orange-vested Washington State Ferry employees guiding us onto the huge boat. *I've never driven onto a boat before*, I thought, as my little Honda worked its way up the ramp. *I'm here for adventures. Driving my car onto a boat is definitely an adventure.*

I shoehorned my Honda into a side compartment, snuggled up behind a black BMW, in front of a ratty blue pickup, and next to a bland sedan with a family of four in it. Once we'd all set our emergency brakes, I saw that most passengers were getting out of their cars. I followed suit. No sense spending the hour and twenty minutes down here in the dark and cold, even if it did perfectly match my mood.

I sidled and squeezed between the tightly packed cars, follow-ing people to a staircase leading to the floor above. I emerged into a big seating area, with booths along each side. Huge win-dows showed only the blackness of night and the rapidly reced-ing lights of the town of Anacortes. I found an unoccupied table and pulled out my phone, opening up Words with Friends. My brother had just scored 57 points, the turkey.

"Kissy?" I muttered. "That's even a word?"

I thought of Kevin's kisses and died a little inside.

No, enough of that. I wasn't going to grieve, I was going to move on. I sent a triple word score and waited. Within ten min-utes, I'd lost the signal. So much for that distraction. I put the phone away and looked around the deck. It was sparsely filled, the few other passengers reading or chatting quietly, or sleeping. Not much call for the 9:05 ferry on a Wednesday night in No-vember.

I stared out into the night, thinking about what lay ahead.

I didn't know the Brixtons well. Okay, understatement: I didn't know him at all; I knew her in the way a hairdresser knows her client. Selectively, I would say. And yet they had just hired me to caretake their estate on Orcas Island—main house, guesthouse, and five acres of grounds on the water at the far end of West Sound. "You'll do wonderfully, my dear," Diana Brixton had said, clutching my hands in her cool ones as she glanced back at her husband, Emmett. I had simply nodded, still reeling, still not believing. "We're just so relieved you're available on such short notice. I don't know what possessed Megan to up and quit like that. After only three weeks."

Maybe she found she hated living on a remote northern island in the dead of winter? I'd wondered. Even in Seattle, we only had about eight hours of daylight in the winter months—when the sun bothered to show up at all. The islands would be worse than that, being pretty much next door to Canada. But I was used to it. I was looking forward to it, in fact. It's less upsetting to vanish if you're already in the dark.

I felt more than heard the shift in the giant ferry's engines as it slowed, turning gently. "Now approaching Lopez, Lopez Island," came the crackly announcement. "Drivers, return to your cars; foot passengers, exit from the car deck."

Lopez looked utterly uninhabited; I saw no lights other than one at the tiny dock. And only two people got up and ambled down the stairs.

Now there's *a remote island,* I thought.

Minutes later, we pulled out, only to slow once more for Shaw Island, which looked no more populous than Lopez.

Finally we pulled into the ferry landing at Orcas. At least there were some signs of life here. Through the pounding rain, I saw what looked like a few stores, maybe a restaurant, and then we were told to return to our cars.

I followed the long line of cars up and out of the big boat, across a steel grate, and then onto the island itself. A sign proclaimed "Orcas Village," but any actual village apparently consisted of two stores, a shuttered ice cream shop, and a charming old hotel; within thirty seconds, I was driving along a winding rural road that held no sign of habitation. In the deep dark, I could not see the printed directions on the card Mrs. Brixton had given me—"Cell service is spotty on the island," she'd said, "so just follow these." My wiper blades thrashed against the rain, barely keeping up.

I drove along with the rest of the ferry traffic, struggling to figure out where I was. Was that a road sign? But it was lost to the rain and the night. Cars turned off onto side roads or private drives, impossible to tell which. No, this couldn't be right; I should have long since turned left at Deer Harbor Road.

There was no shoulder. I drove on, looking for any place to pull over. Finally I parked in a mud-and-gravel driveway in front of a closed gate, hoping the homeowners weren't three cars behind me, anxious to get home and annoyed at my intrusion. I waited a minute to make sure, listening to the rain beat down on the roof of my car. Traffic dwindled and then died away altogether.

I was alone in the dark on an island in the middle of...nowhere.

With a damp sigh, I turned on the dome light and studied Mrs. Brixton's directions. Yes, I was only meant to have gone a half-mile or so on Orcas Road before turning. It was obviously time for the GPS after all.

But when I pulled out my phone, I saw a "Welcome to Canada! International roaming charges may apply!" message on the screen. "What?" I muttered, swiping it open. The message vanished, but my connection icon spun and spun, grabbing a moment of one-bar before flashing "no signal."

"Crap," I said, biting back tears of frustration. Why did everything have to be so impossible? It was late, I was exhausted and hungry and lost. I just wanted to get somewhere warm and dry. Why was this so *hard?*

After a minute, I recovered a few shreds of my equilibrium. Freaking out wasn't going to help anything. I studied the map carefully, trying to memorize the turns and the road names before I turned the car around and drove slowly back down Orcas Road.

This time, I found the sign for Deer Harbor Road. I turned right and followed the narrow road as it wound through the darkness. I passed a small marina; the road rose a bit after that, but I still thought there was water to my left.

I slowed down when the numbers I could see on mailboxes got closer to the Brixtons' address. Even so, I almost drove past it in the dark and rain.

"Wow," I whispered, pulling into the estate's long gravel driveway, stopping at a pair of tall iron gates. The gates were sturdy and new, surrounded by dense landscaping, and lit with bright up-lights; the gravel beneath my wheels looked fresh and clean, and not just from the rain. It was impressive—from what I could see, anyway, which wasn't much.

Studying the card again, I punched a complicated code into the keypad, soaking my arm completely in the process. After a ponderous half-minute, the gates rolled apart smoothly.

I didn't see the house till I was a quarter mile farther, or more, down the driveway. It, too, was lit strategically, highlighting what was probably supposed to look like a cozy, bungalow-style dwelling, just a little beach house. Except that bungalows aren't generally six thousand square feet, and they are *never* three stories high.

I parked out front; I'd figure out the garage and the rest of the grounds tomorrow, when I could see, and when maybe it wouldn't be pouring like this. For now, I just wanted to get inside, eat some dinner, and crash.

My key worked effortlessly in the lock; the door opened with only the sound of the alarm system's *disable me now* chirp, which stopped after I punched in the second code. "Wow," I said again. My voice echoed across the palatial space. The entryway alone was bigger than any apartment I'd ever rented in Seattle. And you could have comfortably put a whole additional floor between my head and the ceiling. I felt like Alice in Wonderland after the "drink me" bottle, shrunk to doll-size in this absurdly large house.

I dropped my wet backpack on the tiled entryway floor, then bent and unbuckled my red rain boots, kicking them off so I wouldn't track mud through the place as I explored the first floor. I found a formal dining room, several parlors, a truly ridiculous number of bathrooms, and a game room, all appointed with barely used furniture, pristine rugs, gorgeous pictures on the walls and sculptures placed strategically where awestruck normal people like myself wouldn't bump into them while wandering, dazzled by the beauty.

At last I found the kitchen, sleek and gleaming, big enough to run a restaurant out of. Alas, it was entirely bare: a stainless steel Sub-Zero fridge so clean it might have been delivered new yesterday; cupboards without so much as a packet of ramen or a tin of sardines. Whoever this mysterious Megan was, she had left nothing behind when she ran off to wherever she'd gone.

The frosted animal cookies I'd gotten out of the vending machine on the ferry would have to do for dinner, then. I'd go to the little town of Eastsound in the morning, find the grocery store, stock up. My stomach grumbled. I got a pristine leaded crystal glass out of an immaculate cupboard and filled it with water from the fridge door. It was very cold, and very wet.

Mrs. Brixton had told me I was welcome to live in the house itself—except when the family was in residence, of course, whereupon I should repair to the guesthouse—but she hadn't specified which bedroom. Silly me: I'd imagined it would be obvious. Didn't normal houses have *a* guest room, like, one? Plus, maybe, a foldout couch for overflow company if you were lucky, or a lumpy futon if you were not so lucky?

The second floor here was like a hotel, with a dizzying array of bedrooms—six, I finally determined, doubling back to make sure I'd seen them all. They were nearly identical, differing only in their gentle shades of decorator colors, containing nary a scrap of personal effects. Each bedroom had its own bathroom. Each bathroom had a generous supply of unopened toothbrushes and full-sized tubes of toothpaste, a variety of fancy shampoos and conditioners and soaps and body washes, several different kinds of disposable razors. Band-Aids and minor first aid items. Lotions and gels and creams and unguents. Feminine supplies. Fascinating: if caretaking didn't work out, I could build my own Walgreen's.

I climbed to the third floor. Aha, here must be where the family lived. There was an obvious master suite taking up most of the front of the house, the sleeping room of which contained an emperor-sized bed, two monstrous dressers, and a cedar chest. The suite had double bathrooms (so *many* bathrooms in this house!), and a closet I could have lived in happily till the end of my days—it even had an adorable little dormer window. The back side of the third floor was divided into two smaller suites. The right-hand one must belong to the daughter—what was her name? Carrie? Something like that. At least this room had some personality—eighties rock posters tacked into the dark-painted walls, a captain's bed, an arrangement of ceramic animal figurines on one of the windowsills.

I walked back down the hall to the second small suite. Ooh, obviously the son's room. Wow. It was the most, er, heavily personalized room in the whole place. Heavy Baroque furniture crowded the capacious space, an achievement in itself. The bed was not only draped in crimson bedding; it had a full-on canopy, also crimson, its heavy side fabric draping to puddle on the floor. Thick, plush wine-dark carpet caressed my toes. A giant roll-top desk stood against the far wall; it could have doubled as a coffin, it was so long. A faint scent of marijuana hung in the air. Clearly, the home of a young prince.

"Whoa," I said, easing the door shut behind me. I just…did not want to know any more about what I might find in that room.

I went back down to the second floor, and chose a room more or less at random, at the back of the house. Its walls were painted a cheery yellow, the bed was made up with a fluffy down comforter, and the windows looked like they might have a view of the water during the day. Good enough. Resisting the urge to unroll a ball of string behind me (not that I had any string, but it was an idea), I went downstairs and back out into the rain to get what I might need out of the car to see me through the night.

Then, with nothing better to do, I decided to turn in. "Home sweet home," I said, pulling back the covers.

Nobody answered.

I was so tired, I hardly cried at all before falling asleep.

❧

I'm an early riser. It's my curse—well, one of them, anyway. No matter how late I get to bed, I'm awake by five, eyes wide open and brain eager to get going. I long ago gave up trying to fight it.

This far north, this late in the year, the sun wouldn't rise for nearly three more hours. But I got up anyway, lingering in the shower a good long time for another good long cry before pulling on some clothes and heading down to that vast, sterile, empty kitchen. Sadly, it was as bare as it had been last night. And I strongly doubted anything in Eastsound would be open this early—especially in the off-season.

"You couldn't even have packed *coffee?*" I grumbled to myself. But no, I'd left Kevin everything, taking only my clothes and books.

At least the rain had stopped during the night. I wandered around the ground floor of the ridiculously huge house again, peering out through the windows. There: a glimmer of light, just starting to touch the horizon. I might as well explore the property.

I pulled on my rain boots and went out the back door, hesitating for a moment before leaving it unlocked behind me. The security measures at this place were extraordinary, and I wasn't sure I could follow them all before caffeine had done its work.

The yard sloped gently downward, leading to what looked like a small private dock below. Picking my way down the muddy terrain, I glanced around at the landscaping. Was I supposed to take care of this too? Not that there was much going on during the winter—rhododendrons, azaleas, the dormant (I hoped) carpet of a lawn. Wouldn't Mrs. Brixton have mentioned it and given me detailed instructions about whatever incredibly complex and expensive bespoke riding mower I'd be using?

I made a note to add this to my list of questions for her.

The sky was lightening just a little more by the time I made it to the dock. It wasn't nearly as grand as the house. It was maybe even a little *weathered*. But it looked like it was in good repair, with berths for four boats, and I felt relief that it didn't need any codes or keys. There was only a humble rowboat tied up now, covered with faded blue canvas, its oars shipped.

I walked out onto the pier, admiring the first glimmers of daylight on the smooth water, looking across at the land I could see—that was still Orcas, right? The next peninsula over? I thought so, though I knew the islands were close together; that could be Shaw. Or Crane? I'd have to get a map, figure out where I was in relation to everything else. All in good time. For now, I simply admired the view. It was gorgeous: rich, dark green hills rising out of the shimmering water, stillness and green, the fresh smell of saltwater and the fresher smell of evergreens, cedar and fir and pine, on the neighboring property. *This* was why I had come here. Away from the madness of the city, here was where I would find my center. Every morning, I would rise, walk down here, and silently commune with daybreak. Water, land, peace, quiet.

The ripping sound of an outboard motor rudely broke the morning's stillness.

Oh well. I stood on the pier and watched a small motorboat chug into the bay, cutting its engine as it cruised closer to shore. Aboard was one man, a ball cap pulled low on his head. Was he planning to dock here? No, at the last minute the boat disappeared into a stand of trees to the southwest of me. Maybe he was a neighbor; next door, or maybe a few houses down.

The engine slowed further, and fell silent. I watched the ripples of the boat's wake spread and eventually settle back into the quiet motion of the bay. The boat was gone, the water the only sound I heard. I could relax. I would regain my mood, I would return to that quiet place where I could be present and calm and at peace with being alone for the rest of my life, because I was unfit for relationships and doomed to fail every time I tried to have one.

I saw where this was going. But I didn't cry.

The daylight was gathering; a glance at my watch told me it was past seven-thirty. Maybe, just maybe, there would be a coffee shop in town, and maybe it would open at eight. If not, at least the grocery store should. My stomach grumbled, louder and more insistent than last night. Those animal cookies were a fond memory from ancient days.

As I stepped off the pier and back onto the path, I heard voices through the trees. The man who had come in off the boat, it must be; there was a woman's voice too. I'm reserved by nature, but I'm also practical. Knowing my neighbors would be a good idea in a house this remote. And, hey, they might have coffee. I decided to introduce myself. It would be good. Normal, even. Thus girded, I walked over toward the property line, a little surprised not to see a fence.

"Well?" The woman's voice stopped me in my tracks, still in the thick trees. The word was barked out; the anger in it was unmistakable. Whoever she was, she was pissed. "You were supposed to take care of this for me."

Oh no. Was I going to live next door to one of those fighting couples?

I could see them. Her back was mostly toward me, so I couldn't see her face, but the man from the boat stood, hands outspread, his face a study in tried patience. "Come on, Sheila, just calm down, babe. Put that thing away."

"Like I'm supposed to trust you? Seriously, Gregory?" The woman was still, her arm extended, pointing at him. But not her finger...oh no, was she holding a *gun*?

I stifled a gasp and felt my skin crawl, the familiar tingle and hammer behind my skin as I vanished, chameleoning into the dappled shade. I couldn't move.

Gregory's voice shifted from condescending to wheedling. "Aw, come on, babe. If you don't have it, I can wait a *little* while. As long as you give me what you owe me."

"I've *given you* plenty," she hissed. "You forget, it's my neck on the line here."

"All right. One more day, but that's it. Now put that thing away."

"Not even a little chance," she snarled. "After I covered for you? What you *did?*" She continued to hold the gun on the man, shaking her head. "No more."

"Look. I don't like your tone. You forget, two can play your game."

She shook her head. "That's a dumb thing to say to someone holding a gun." There was a pause. A tiny "pop." A puff of smoke out of the muzzle of the gun, rising softly as the man crumpled to the ground.

Forcing myself back into motion, I stuffed my hand into my mouth to avoid screaming. My skin crawled and stung; my heart pounded. *Oh man oh man oh man*, I thought. *She just killed that guy.* He lay motionless on the ground. She glanced around, looking right through me as, trembling, I dropped to my knees in the mud.

Thank goodness for mud. Soft, quiet mud.

CHAPTER 2

As I huddled, frozen with fear, in the shade of the trees, the woman shoved the gun into a coat pocket, pulled out a cell phone, and began walking away. I heard her say something into the phone, someone's name? I had to get out of there before she could see me. Was she really going away? Still struggling for control, I forced myself back to my feet, then staggered as quietly as I could back up to the Brixton house. I kept to the trees as much as possible, stepping softly, my heart hammering.

I slipped in the door, closing it silently behind me. I pulled off my boots, rubbed at my arms, brushed the mud off my jeans, paced and shivered. *I have to call the cops* I wanted to say, but my voice was gone, crushed into silence by panic and confusion.

I just saw a murder. I repeated it silently. Trying to make it real. How could it be real?

Standing in the kitchen, I cleared my throat. There: a tiny bit of voice. I tried, "Hello." Just audible. Maybe. I pulled out my cell phone, walked over to the window where the signal was better, and dialed 911.

"San Juan Sheriff's office," came the extremely pleasant voice on the other end of the line. "What is your emergency?"

To my intense relief, I found I could speak again. Well, it was more of a croak, but I could be heard, my voice was no longer stripped away. "I just saw a man get shot at, on..." *where am I?* "...on Deer Harbor Road."

"Orcas?"

"Yeah."

"One moment." There was a pause, the sound of keys clicking, maybe the muffled crackle of a radio in the background. "Your name?"

"Camille Tate. I'm caretaking on Deer Harbor. I just saw a shooting..."

"Are you in a safe place?"

"Yes! I got—I'm in the house. I mean next door. I, uh..." I could feel my tears rising, threatening to close my throat. To silence me again. "I'm safe, I think."

"Okay. That's good. Hold on a moment." More clicking of keys. "Are you near the victim?"

"No! I ran—"

"Tell me the address you're at, ma'am."

I rattled off the Brixtons' address, getting it wrong twice before getting it right. "Sorry," I added. "I just moved here yesterday."

"Yesterday." More clicking of keys, then the radio again, as my dispatcher talked to someone. Numbers and codes and jargon, almost inaudible. "Okay, we're sending a boat around, and a car. Someone should be there within ten minutes."

Ten minutes? What had I gotten myself into, where it took police ten minutes to get to the scene of a murder? "Oh, no, it's not here—it's next door. From here. I don't know their address. But the, uh, boat and car, they should go there."

"Next door?"

"The next place over, farther down the road, from here. South, I think? Or west? I'm sorry, I..."

"That's all right, ma'am."

"Do I, uh, have to be there? I mean, when they...?"

"No, you should stay clear of the gunman, but we'll want to be able to find you to answer any questions."

"Woman."

"Excuse me?"

"You said gunman. But it was a woman. Who did the shooting. The guy called her Sheila. The guy who got shot." I was taken over by shivering again, and felt my skin crawl. But I had to stay here, I had to stay present. No fading away. The police were on their way.

"I see." The voice grew muffled again, as if the dispatcher pulled her mouthpiece away to talk to someone else. Then, "Please stay put, Ms. Tate. Someone will be by soon."

"Okay."

"Do you want me to stay on the line until someone arrives?"

"No. Thank you. I'm good."

"All right." She hung up. I put my cell phone down on the precious marble-topped end table, not even realizing till now that I'd paced my way out of the kitchen and into the big, grand living room. Alice again. Had I really fallen down the rabbit-hole? I was just glad the call hadn't dropped.

I was still waiting for my skin to feel normal, for my body to stop shaking uncontrollably. I kept up my pacing throughout the entire first floor of the house while I waited for the next thing to happen.

❧

Two hours later, a nice, clean-cut, good-looking young man in a crisp khaki uniform kept telling me that nothing had happened.

I mean, not in so many words. Deputy Rankin questioned me carefully, thoroughly, and politely. He wrote down everything I said in a spiral notebook, even though he'd also set up a little portable tape recorder on the kitchen counter between us. He took me through the whole story, from the boat arriving, to the argument, to the obviously silenced gunshot, to the man crumpling to the ground, to Sheila's phone call afterwards. I told him I was hidden by the trees, that I didn't think either Sheila or her victim had seen me. The deputy clearly already had information from whoever he had talked to next door. I couldn't tell from his professionally blank demeanor whether I was confirming or contradicting that information.

After he got the whole story, he carefully questioned me about myself: why I was here, what I had done before, what was my relationship to the Brixtons. And he did all of this in a voice so pleasant, so calming, that I couldn't help but calm down myself.

"All right, thank you very much," he said, shutting the notebook and getting calmly, unhurriedly, to his feet. Ever so calm, all of it. There had been no sirens, no unusual activity next door, no ambulance or coroner's van or *anything*. If a boat had arrived, it had done so quietly. Calmly.

I got up too. "But…that's it? What about…"

He gave me a gentle smile. "Yes, Ms. Tate?"

I felt my skin begin to tingle just a little. "Did you find…a body? Did you find that woman, and arrest her?"

His smile slipped, just a bit. But his tone was as gracious as ever. "I'm afraid I am not able to share details of any ongoing investigation, Ms. Tate. But…just between you and me, you have no reason to feel unsafe here."

I stood firm. "But…"

He sighed, pausing a moment before obviously coming to some decision. "The owner of the estate next door is the founder of a local repertory theater. The troupe often rehearses on the grounds. It seems that you witnessed an unusually realistic bit of play-acting."

"Play-acting?"

"There's a lot of it goes on next door. You've landed in a very creative community." He smiled at me once more, and handed me a business card. "Here's our non-emergency number, for the future. We like to keep the 911 lines free for real trouble."

"I…" I stammered, feeling my face color. "Of course."

"Though naturally, if you have an emergency, you should always feel free to dial 911."

"I will." At least my skin had settled back down. I set the white card down on the vast countertop. It looked as small as I felt. I wasn't sure how much more of an idiot I could be. Hopefully I wouldn't find out, or I'd have to move away in humiliation. "I'm sorry."

"There is no need to apologize."

My brain continued to struggle with the information. "You said…that was…theater?"

"Yes." His smile was now entirely genuine. "Orcas is a very artistic place; our theater is extremely high-quality. We get a lot of Seattle actors out here—and we even had a guy from Broadway a few years ago. I think the next play is *Murder For Two*. You might want to check it out."

I shook my head, hugely embarrassed and deeply confused. "All right. Thank you, Deputy Rankin."

"You're welcome, Ms. Tate."

"I'm sorry you had to come out here for…for nothing. I'd at least offer to make you some coffee, but there isn't any. I haven't even been to Eastsound yet."

"Not a problem. You're free to do that now if you like." He smiled and touched the bill of his sheriff's department cap. "And welcome to Orcas Island."

Well, way to make an absolute fool of myself before I've been here twelve hours, I thought, as I watched his newish, shiny SUV rumble back up the gravel driveway toward the road.

It had seemed so real. Which, of course, was the point, right? Actors. Acting. Creating a false reality for the benefit of an audience. Something I should maybe know about, since I wanted to write a screenplay?

I was completely mortified, and I hadn't even had breakfast.

I took a deep breath. Obviously this paranoid city chick had some things to learn about life on a remote island full of creative types. It was long past time to get to town for some coffee. And groceries too, of course. But definitely coffee.

ᏋᏏ

I had just punched the code to close the gates behind me and was about to pull out when I saw a woman hailing me from the road. I took the car out of gear and rolled the window back down.

She walked toward me, unhurried, smiling. It wasn't Sheila, the woman who'd "shot" the guy—this one was slightly older than me, or maybe a lot older and super well preserved. She had an expensive, cared-for look to her, adapted for a Pacific Northwest island environment. Honey blond hair that had been blown dry and moussed into an artfully tousled mop; a Pendleton plaid shirt over an expensive base-layer tee; perfectly broken-in Levi's; low-rise Trek walking boots.

"Hi!" she called out, as she got closer.

I smiled back. "Hi."

"I'm Lisa Cannon," she said, reaching the car and putting out a fine-boned hand. Short clean nails, no rings. "I'm your neighbor."

I reached out through the car window, awkwardly, and shook her hand. "Camille Tate. Or Cam."

She glanced down toward the Brixtons' estate, hidden in the trees behind me. "You're the new caretaker?"

"Yep." And, sparing her the need to work up to it casually, I added, "I'm so sorry. It was me. I called the cops. I was out on the dock and saw the rehearsal and I thought it was a real murder."

She laughed, fine lines crinkling attractively at the corners of her grey eyes. "Oh, what a welcome for you! My apologies. I'm afraid we sometimes forget we're not alone out here."

"Not a problem," I said, because that's what you're supposed to say when people pretend to kill each other in front of you but it was all in fun. Right? But in truth, I was basking in my relief. It wasn't as if I'd *wanted* to witness a murder. Talk about complicating your whole day. "I'm sorry you had to deal with all that."

She gave a gentle shrug. "It's always nice to spend a few hours with Deputy Rankin." Then she looked at my car, her expression politely not registering how shabby it was. "But I can see you're headed out—I just wanted to say hi, and to invite you over for a glass of wine and a snack, maybe this evening." She studied me a moment. "You do drink wine?"

"Yes, gladly, though at the moment I'm in search of coffee."

She laughed again, joyful and natural. "Ah, someone with her priorities straight! Well, I won't keep you. Five, five-thirty? The gate will be open, just walk on down."

"Sure."

As I pulled out, I glanced in the rearview mirror. Lisa Cannon walked back down the side of the road toward her own estate, looking relaxed, arms swinging gently by her sides.

I wasn't a naturally outgoing person. In fact, I tended to keep to myself, for obvious reasons. My present state of solitude was appealing, but I wanted to know *someone* here. I felt ridiculously isolated. I thought I'd like that after trying to live peacefully with Kevin. But it was too much, I realized.

I at least needed someone I could turn to in case I ran out of coffee and the store was closed. And I *had* wanted to meet the neighbors, after all.

❧

The drive to Eastsound was just gorgeous. Adorable little farms—I saw an "eggs for sale" sign, and a herd of goats; gentle rolling hills leading down to perfectly placed ponds; the tidy harbor I'd driven past last night, at West Sound. Snowy mountains in the distance. It was hard to keep my eyes on the road.

The low winter light revealed a landscape that couldn't have been more charming if someone had designed it, inch by inch, to illustrate a children's book.

In all the years I'd lived in Seattle, how had I never made it out to the San Juans?

I drove up Crow Valley Road, and then joined a traffic-free Orcas Road—the main road from the ferry, where I'd gotten so lost last night. Today, everything seemed so straightforward. Well, it is easier when you can see.

Eastsound itself sat at the top of the long, skinny bay—well, sound—from which it took its name. "Wow," I said yet again, as I pulled into a parking spot with a million-dollar view. I stood by the car and just marveled for a minute, watching the water shimmer in the slight breeze, wondering if anyone lived on that tiny dot of land just offshore (was it its own island? Did it have a name?). I then dragged my eyes away from the view and proceeded to explore the booming metropolis of Eastsound on foot. It took all of five minutes: one street parallel to the sound and two perpendicular ones comprised much of the central business district. Most businesses were closed, however. Early hour? It was after ten. Shuttered for the winter, maybe? That would be too bad.

The Island Market on Prune Alley was open. It looked to be a regular grocery store, and sat next to a divey-looking bar called the Lower Tavern. Wait, was the Tavern open? In the *morning*? I smelled something maybe like nachos and certainly like beer; my stomach growled demandingly. But back by my car was the Brown Bear Bakery, on the corner of Main and North Beach Streets. I hiked back there, hearing the blessed sounds of an espresso machine from half a block away.

Oh, yes.

Inside, the bakery smelled amazing. My vending-machine and cold-water dinner had been inadequate even at the time; now I thought I might faint before I could get my mouth around a giant sugar-topped chocolate muffin and a triple latte.

At last, I had sustenance.

I took a seat on one of the high metal barstools that looked out onto Main Street. Appealing little shops across the street caught my eye—Darvill's bookstore, a pottery store, a cute knickknack shop, an Irish pub. All good. All to be checked out once I was settled and comfortable here (and once they were open) (if they ever opened). For now, I nibbled the muffin and savored the coffee. I ordered a second muffin to go, after eyeing—and resisting—the bread pudding and the quiche. Small victories count, yes? And I could have those another day, preferably a payday. This island may have been more adorable than Seattle, but it certainly wasn't any cheaper.

That realization was only underlined ten minutes later in the Island Market. "Six dollars for a pint of ice cream?" I muttered to myself. Good gracious. I'd thought the Brixtons were paying me handsomely for what basically amounted to living in a huge house and attempting to work on a screenplay. At these prices, though, I might have to hang out my hairdresser's shingle, or maybe get a waitressing gig, just to eat.

Back at the estate, I put my carefully selected groceries away (for some reason, baby bok choy had been only sixty-nine cents a bag; I'd bought nearly a bushel), and then puttered around the house for a bit, making sure I'd seen all the rooms during my explorations last night. As a caretaker, I had to find some caring to do, so I checked to see that taps weren't running and lights weren't left on anywhere. Caretaking; I was caretaking. Best darn caretaker ever: that was me.

That done, it was time to learn more about my new environment. Walking boots on, free tourist map I'd gotten at the grocery store in hand, I set out down Deer Harbor Road in the direction of the West Sound harbor. It had looked like there might be a few little businesses there—a bed & breakfast, maybe even a restaurant.

The day was still chilly; I had on my heaviest sweater, a Seattle thrift-store score, made in Norway. It was heavy enough to qualify as outerwear. I pulled it more tightly around me and walked faster, stepping off the road onto the gravel shoulder when the occasional car ambled by.

I passed a discreet sign pointing toward a trailhead. I love to hike, so I'd be investigating that later. There were a few vacation rental cottages, windmills, more goats and what looked to be a closed farm stand. After about fifteen minutes of walking, I made the harbor. Yes: both a B&B and a restaurant, and…both closed for the season.

I stood in the restaurant's parking lot, peering forlornly through its windows. Chairs were up on tables; a wooden bar looked spacious, inviting, and completely inaccessible.

Fine. I'd return to the vast estate for a plate of scrambled eggs and bok choy. And that second muffin.

The crunch of a footstep on gravel behind me made me turn; the sight made me stifle a gasp, stand up straight, and wonder if I'd remembered to brush my hair before I left the house this morning. "Hello," said the most gorgeous vision of a man I'd ever seen outside of a calendar.

I barely kept myself from saying "wow" yet again, even though the sheer magnitude of his good looks made me irritated. Men that lovely—it just wasn't fair, wasn't right. They made me uncomfortable (I know: what didn't?). I tried not to scowl. "Uh… hello?"

The vision smiled, and became human, though still insanely good-looking. Dark hair, just a little shaggy; warm brown eyes; strong, athletic build, a plaid flannel shirt tucked into just-tight-enough jeans underneath a short fleece jacket. "Restaurant's closed."

"I noticed."

He put out a callused, oil-stained hand. "Colin."

I shook it. His skin was rough, but warm. "Cam. I just moved here."

"Figured." Colin smiled again. Oh come on. A person could

lose herself in those brown eyes if she was inclined to, and I most definitely was not. "You don't have the tourist look to you."

"I don't? What does a tourist look like?"

Now he laughed, and shrugged. "Can't explain it. It's just— well, live here long enough, you can see it."

Probably tourists brushed their hair. I gave mine a toss and resented the fact that I was expected to make conversation, before reminding myself that it was good to meet the neighbors, be friendly to folks, even when they were ruggedly handsome to an absurd degree.

He dragged his hand through his own mop of hair. "You been here long?"

"Going on fourteen hours, I think. You?"

"All my life." He motioned to the harbor below. "Working boats now, repairs. Run sailboat tours in season, a little whale-watching."

"I guess you get to see a lot of tourists that way."

"Sure do." Now he shrugged, suddenly self-conscious. "Well, just passing by. Saw you looking through the window. Thought you might be lost."

Only now did I see a beat-up red pickup idling by the side of Crow Valley Road. "Oh, no, not lost. I'm caretaking down the road, and was just trying to get a feel for the neighborhood. Such as it is."

"Caretaking? Where?"

"Up the road a bit."

He nodded. "Got it."

I'd put him off. But I didn't want to be a jerk. He was just being friendly. Neighborly. Right? "The Brixtons' place, do you know it?"

He gave me an unreadable look, then nodded. "Sure do."

"So, uh, yeah. That's where I am. At the Brixtons'. Down the road." I smiled at him.

What was I doing? Was I actually trying to flirt with him? I was terrible at flirting, at small talk. Besides, a man I loved had just dumped me. I'd cried more since yesterday than I had in the last ten years. I had a broken heart. Not flirting. Was I? Was this just something that happened automatically because this man was so handsome?

Ugh.

I was not interested in him, but apparently he thought I was because he grinned again. "Well, welcome to the neighborhood. Guess I should bring you a casserole." His gaze caught mine. "Maybe buy you a drink sometime?"

I had my excuse at the ready. "I have a—" *No I don't. Not anymore.* "I mean, I, I—"

"Got it."

"No! You don't—I just…had a relationship end. Badly." I found myself blinking back sudden tears. I'd gone from inadvertent flirt to total basket case in what, ten seconds? "I'm, you know, taking some time."

"Understood." Now his smile flashed again. "Back to the casserole idea, then."

I gave a sort of strangled warble, the sound of a laugh forcing its way past the lump in my throat. "Thanks. I love casserole. But just, you know. Casserole."

"Sure." We stood staring awkwardly at one another. I felt my skin begin to tingle. *No, no!* I thought, and took a step backward. *He's not a threat. He's a vision of exquisite small town masculinity, and he's flirting. Calm down, Cam.* The tingling remained, very faint.

But he'd noticed my step back. "Well, I gotta get along," he said. "Nice to meet you, Cam."

"You too, Colin."

I waited until the red pickup had motored away before I smacked my forehead with the flat of my hand. "Stupid, Camille! *I love casserole?* Jeez." But as much as I hated the fact that I'd dissolved into feeble remarks about my ruined relationship and goofball burbles about food, I was glad. I'd been so strange, there was no way this man would pursue anything with me. I was, after all, a complete emotional mess. Not looking for someone new. The only connections I wanted on this island were friendly connections.

Even though he was possibly the best-looking man I'd ever seen.

I mean especially because of that.

It was faint, but my skin still tingled, pricking my arms with tiny waves of stinging shivers. Colin was gone, the lane was empty. But there was a threat here.

I wondered where it was hiding.

CHAPTER 3

What does one wear to have a glass of wine with one's new neighbor who definitely didn't have a murder on her property this morning? I didn't know, but my options were limited, so, taking my cue from what I'd seen her wear earlier, I chose clean jeans and my only cashmere sweater. Italian, long staple because it never pilled, 100% cashmere—also, I'd like to add, an amazing thrift store score. Though I probably wouldn't tell that part to Lisa Cannon.

Her estate was even more elaborate and spectacular than the Brixtons', and even less visible from the road—a perfect secluded hideaway. From what I could tell as I walked down the long driveway, she had a huge main house, plus several outbuildings, any one of which would have been a million-dollar home in Seattle, even without the property underneath.

Or the view. "Come in," Lisa said at the door, flashing her warm golden smile. She led me down a few steps into a bright, glowing space—a sunken living room, all glass walls angled out onto the bay, catching the last of the sunset. The rays bounced and dazzled, making something of a crucible for my eyes.

I blinked, nearly unable to see the steps or the furniture or my hostess over the glare. "Gorgeous view."

"Yes—sorry about the sun, but we see so little of it in the winter, I like to make the most of it."

"No, it's great. Dazzling, in fact." My eyes almost hurt.

She showed me to a plush couch and took a chair across from it. An unlabeled bottle of something red and two glasses sat on a low table between us. She lifted the bottle. "May I?"

"Yes, thank you."

She poured out the ruby-colored liquid, then handed me a glass before pouring her own. "A blend, mostly Cabernet Franc, made by a friend who has a little winery in the Rattlesnake Hills."

"Oh," I said, sniffing at the wine, pretending like I knew what she was talking about. It smelled fantastic.

She lifted her glass to mine. As we clinked, she said, "To new neighbors!"

"To new neighbors."

I sipped, then quickly took another, bigger sip. "Wow, this is amazing! Your friend should sell this!"

Lisa gave her tinkling, delighted laugh. "Ah, he does; but largely to…particular restaurants. I don't imagine you would know the label."

I didn't imagine I would either, but Kevin probably would have. He loved wine, and was always trying to coach me on which notes I should taste.

Kevin. I felt tears spring up behind my eyelids.

I could have cursed. I really didn't want to sit in my neighbor's palatial living room and cry, so I quietly concentrated on the complexity of what was going on in my mouth. It was distractingly delicious. The wine slipped down my throat as the sun slipped below the horizon; the rays stopped bouncing and glowing and burning my eyes, and I could finally see the room a lot better.

I glanced around, taking in the décor. Bright and spare and modern. The chair Lisa sat on was leather, cream-colored, and just slightly asymmetrical; a large abstract oil painting hung over a fireplace big enough to roast a whole pig in. Again, I realized how much more substantial this house was than the Brixtons'. Which, yesterday, I wouldn't have thought was possible.

"I don't know a lot about wine," I admitted. "I'm sure I couldn't afford this. But it's delicious."

She gave me a kind smile. "So!" she said, setting her glass on the marble-topped table between us. "Tell me a little about yourself, Camille. What brings you to Orcas?"

Reluctantly, I set my own glass down too, before I could make a jerk of myself guzzling the whole thing. "Well, I needed a change. Diana Brixton is a client, and she told me they'd just lost their caretaker suddenly, and wondered if I might be interested. I took it as a sign from the universe. Caretaking sounded interesting, and like something I could do. And the remote-island part sounded really cool. So…here I am."

"A client for what?"

"I do hair. Like, on your head? But I'm hoping to write a screenplay while I'm out here."

Lisa smiled brightly and leaned forward, as though I'd just told her the most fascinating tidbit of information ever. "A screenplay! What about?"

I shrugged, feeling self-conscious as always. My skin gave a little tingle; I quickly took another sip of the wine. Alcohol always calmed everything down. It relaxed me enough that my fears dissipated, so I loved it and was careful of it at the same time. "When you do hair, you hear so many stories. I always thought I should write them down, or…use them somehow."

She nodded, tossing her own well-kempt hair slightly. "Oh, the salon as confessional. Yes, what marvelous material you must get—a treasure trove. When I think of the things I tell my stylist!" She laughed. "I should have had her sign an NDA years ago!"

"What do you do?" I asked, wondering just how a person afforded such an astonishing house. Was there a rich husband hidden here somewhere? "I mean, besides the theater?"

"I'm retired, mostly." At my blank look (could she be even much past forty?), she went on. "I had a little tech company in Seattle. I stepped back when I decided I wanted to live out here full-time."

A little tech company? I thought. *Little compared to Microsoft?* "Ah."

"But the theater is truly my passion," she said, taking another sip of her wine. "And the actors out here are *so* talented, such a joy to work with. They really do lose themselves in their roles. I'm sorry again for the scare this morning."

"Oh, that's all right."

"They had no idea anyone saw them! They were completely immersed in rehearsal." She gave me a smile. "You must have been quiet as a mouse."

"I, uh, there were shadows, and the ground was pretty soft. I didn't want to bother them." *Well, except for the whole call-ing-the-police part!* Chagrined, I felt my heart beating faster, and cast about for a change of subject. "Do you live here alone?"

"Yes, mostly, though the actors do come and go. As you no-ticed this morning." Again, the bright smile. "I know it's rather too much space for one person. But after the big city, it just feels so freeing."

I thought of the last place I'd lived in Seattle. A tiny studio, shared with Kevin. Jam-packed with character and everything else, it was charming, cramped, and way too expensive.

No place to hide.

"Yes, the island is gorgeous," I said. "I explored a bit this morn-ing."

"Did you get down to Rosario?"

"No—I just drove into Eastsound, and then walked around here a bit after that."

She leaned in again, grey eyes bright. "You must go tour the Rosario Mansion! It's fantastic, and quite strange. And if you hike, the views from Mt. Constitution are not to be believed…"

I'm not much of a talker, but somehow we chatted comfortably. I sipped more wine, which helped as wine always does. Before I knew it, an hour had gone by and Lisa was rising to her feet. "I'd ask you to stay to dinner, but I'm afraid I'm already engaged for the evening."

"Oh!" I got up as well, glancing sadly at the unlabeled bottle. "No, that's fine—I have a house full of groceries. Thank you for the wine."

"Thank you for taking the time to share it with me." She started walking me to the door, then stopped at a small side table and opened its single drawer. "Here—my card, with my cell and house phone numbers on it. In case you need anything."

The card was ivory, with raised letters. It said only "Lisa Cannon," and the two numbers. "Thanks—I should give you my cell too." I fumbled in my purse for a piece of scratch paper, not finding anything. "I don't have cards…"

"Just tell it to me. I'll remember it."

"Really?"

"I've a very good memory." She gave me a calm smile.

And then I was walking back to the Brixtons', slightly buzzed, shaking my head in wonderment. *What an interesting place this island is.*

❧

When I got back to the Brixtons' front door, I found a small, tidy brown bag leaning against it. It looked safe enough. I picked it up and opened it just enough to smell the deep, toasty notes of artisanal coffee roasting. Who had left it? Who could circumvent the gates and hedges and pass keys of the Brixton place?

I decided that whoever it was, this person was now my new best friend.

But what if it was decaf?

❧

I started my second day on the island with baby bok choy and eggs. I'd barely finished a cup of the delicious mystery coffee when I was seized with energy and purpose.

Definitely not decaf.

I turned my attention to a smallish room on the first floor at the back of the house, beyond the kitchen, with a nice sliver of view down to the dock—enough to be pretty to look at, but not too much to be distracting. I couldn't figure out its purpose. Pantry? But no, there was a big butler's pantry. Maybe houses this big just sort of bred extra rooms when you weren't looking.

Whatever the room was supposed to be for, it would make a perfect writing studio. I dragged in a table from the front parlor and a chair from the dining room, plugged in my laptop, and settled in. I had been surfing the Internet for two hours, drinking more of that heavenly coffee and getting in the right frame of mind to write, when I heard a strange bell.

"What the...?" I got up and walked out into the hallway, listening for it.

It came again. "Oh!" I ran to the entry hall and pushed the intercom button. "Yes?"

"FedEx!"

"Right! Just a moment." I stared at the panel, trying to figure out which button opened the gate. *This one?* I pressed it, and then hit the intercom again. "Did that open it?" I got no response, but I heard an engine a moment later. "Guess so." I opened the front door, only to see an unmarked white panel van coming up the driveway.

"Oh, crap," I muttered. The van rumbled to a stop

How gullible was I? Who had I just let in here? *What's wrong with me?* My skin started to crawl, but calmed when a perky redheaded young woman jumped out, wearing canvas pants and a cable-knit sweater. Her bouncy curls could only be natural; there's nothing you can do with chemicals to get hair to look like that. The color, too.

All her friends must secretly hate her, I thought.

She walked up to me, holding a familiar white envelope, purple and orange block letters across its side. "Oh! FedEx!" I cried, relieved.

The woman gave me a quizzical look as she held out the envelope. "That's what I said. You Camille Tate?"

"Yes."

"Sign here." She handed over a clipboard and a ballpoint pen.

I signed, saying, "But…no uniform…no official truck? And don't you guys usually have those electronic things for signatures?"

Now she laughed. "Not on Orcas. You're pretty suspicious, aren't you?"

I shrugged. I'd buzzed her in, hadn't I? "I'm not from here."

She took back the clipboard. "Thanks! Buzz me out?"

"Oh. Sure."

She rattled back down the driveway. I must have pushed the right button again, because she didn't come back.

I took the envelope inside, back to my "writing studio," and looked at it. The return address was Seattle—oh, Diana Brixton. I pulled the tab, opening it.

Inside was a short handwritten note clipped to a packet of papers.

Dear Camille,

I hope you've found the place all right and that it wasn't too much of a shambles.

I snorted at this, and kept reading.

Enclosed is the house manual. It occurs to me that I have no idea where (or even if) Megan may have left her copy, so I've had another one printed up.

Emmett and the children and I have decided to spend Thanksgiving on the island this year after all. Please ensure that the house is ready for our occupation by Monday the 23rd, though I don't believe anyone will be arriving before Tuesday.

Let me know if you have any questions.
Sincerely,
Diana Brixton

I set the note aside, frowning. Well, so much for my lovely winter of solitude, alone in a giant mansion. The 23rd was only two weeks from now. *Guess I ought to look at the guesthouse,* I thought.

I picked up the hefty house manual and began leafing through it. The thing must have been an inch thick. About a third of the way in, I found a section labeled GROUNDS, and sighed with relief. Apparently a gardening service came twice a week during the summer and once every other week during the winter; the live-in caretaker was only expected to keep an eye on things, water any plants that looked dried out, and call the service if heavier work needed doing.

Of course, Diana was very thorough. She would not have forgotten to mention gardening duties.

Assuming I would have remembered it if she did, I realized. My mind had really not been tracking all that well when I'd met with her and Mr. Brixton; it wasn't doing a whole lot better at the moment. It's a complex process, grief. I should know: I'd done it before.

But this time was supposed to be different...

"Don't go there," I whispered. I knew, *knew* that I couldn't trust anyone. Since my earliest years, I'd known I was different. Normal people didn't...blank out of existence, frozen in place, staring at whatever had threatened them, terrified them, traumatized them.

Erased them. Silenced them.

Silenced *me*. Like the first time.

"Don't go there," I said again, nearly growling this time. "Do. Not. Think. About. It."

Abruptly, I stood up and walked out of the room, yanking my brain almost forcibly from unendurable memories. In the kitchen, I grabbed the ring of keys and went out the back door.

The guesthouse sat about a hundred yards behind and to the left of the main house—on the far side from Lisa Cannon's estate, I noticed—across what was probably a nice lawn in the summertime. The house itself was small compared to the mansion, but they shared the same aesthetic. It was therefore much more adorable: an actual bungalow, rather than the gargantuan imitation of one.

Inside, it was also more modestly furnished, but still pretty nice. And built to a more human scale—no more Alice Syndrome. I walked through the rooms, laughing at myself for resenting being "downsized" into this charming little two-bedroom house. It would have fetched three-quarters of a million on Capitol Hill, easy. And I was getting paid to live here.

The front bedroom would make a perfect office; the back bedroom was at least as comfortable as the one I'd chosen in the main house. There was even a copy of the panel at the front door for controlling the driveway gate, complete with intercom. "All right, moving day," I said to myself, and headed back to the main house for my things.

Fifteen minutes later, I stood before the cottage's fridge, trying to find room for all my baby bok choy. Of course the main house's kitchen was bare: *this* was where Megan had been living. The fridge was full of sauces and jams and bottled water and cheese and some almost-nasty lettuce and an unopened half-gallon of nonfat milk that hadn't reached its expiration date. The freezer even had a small bag of coffee beans, labeled *Local Goods Orcas Roast: Organic Peruvian Dark.* "Thank you, Megan!" I said to the empty space. "Wherever you are." I opened the bag and gave it a sniff. Nice, but not as heavenly as the mystery beans I'd found at the front door of the main house. "Maybe I'll save these for special occasions," I said, stashing the unmarked bag in the freezer.

I found her copy of the house manual, too, peeking out from

under the bed in the back bedroom. It looked hardly touched; I set it on the dresser, next to the one Diana had sent me.

All told, moving house took an hour or so, then another hour to remake the little room in the main house where I'd slept two nights (as if anyone was even going to notice), and to tidy the place up and wash the sheets and towels and get everything ready for the Brixtons.

I was caretaking the heck out of that place, yes I was.

And then there was nothing to do but pretend to work on my screenplay until dinner.

❧

Walking helps spur the creative brain.

I was on my third or ninth or twentieth pass through the house—living room to dining nook to kitchen, a turn into the hall, then back up past the bedroom and the bathroom and the other bedroom, jogging at the corner to avoid the office and its mocking blank Word file—when something white in the fireplace caught my eye. I stopped and pulled aside the metal screen, bending down to look.

Amid the cold ashes and a mostly-burnt log, I saw a crumpled piece of paper, barely scorched. As if it had been thrown into a dying fire, smoldered a bit, but didn't catch. I pulled it out, shaking off ashes before smoothing it flat.

It was part of a sheet of lined paper, obviously from a spiral notebook, torn in half before it was discarded. It took me a minute to decipher the messy, scrawled handwriting.

Gregory—

Call me as soon as you get back. I'm not sure what's going on but I'm scared. I've got a ferry reservation for the Thursday morning sailing, 7:00—come with me, it's not too late. There are people in the city that can help. I talked to Sheila and sh

The note ended midsentence, at the tear.

I stood in the middle of the living room, holding the paper, trying to make sense of it. It had to be Megan who wrote this, right? She'd been the last person living here, before she...left.

Megan knew Gregory? Was she an actor too?

Sheila was the woman with the gun. Gregory, the actor who had been "shot" had called her that. I racked my memory. *"Come on, Sheila, just calm down, babe. Put that thing away."* I could almost hear his voice.

Sheila and Gregory were their actual names, then? But they were rehearsing. Or improvising. Or something. Why had they used their real names, not character names?

A shiver ran through me; I dropped the note, not wanting it in my hands. I could feel a prickle rising along my arms, but I shook it out as I hurried in to my computer, opened the browser, and searched for "theater Orcas Island."

The Orcas Island Repertory Theater popped up; I pulled up its page. Yes, this was the one: "...founded in 2010 by noted philanthropist and theater enthusiast Lisa Cannon...rave reviews both locally and afar..." I scrolled down. *A Green, Green Field* had just closed; *Murder for Two* was opening right after the new year. Yes, the deputy had mentioned that.

That looks like a fun play, but it sure doesn't sound like what they were rehearsing, I thought, reading the description. An Agatha Christie-inspired musical-comedy-murder mystery send-up with a bunch of roles, all played by...two men.

No women at all.

Maybe they'd been working on their *next* play? (Would the theater do two plays in a row about murder?) Maybe they were just, I don't know, brainstorming, practicing, ad-libbing...?

With their real names?

"Nobody was killed," I said aloud, forcing myself to hear it. "Deputy Rankin said it was nothing. Lisa Cannon said it was nothing." I got up and started walking through the house again. "You're just trying to get out of writing," I told myself. "There is *nothing weird going on* here."

On my next pass through the living room, though, I picked up the piece of paper and read it again. Megan was scared. She wanted Gregory to call her as soon as he got back. From where? She wanted him to go away with her. To where? But then…she didn't give him the note. She tore it up and threw it in the fireplace instead.

Where was the other half of the note? I bent down, picking through the ashes again, but it had either burned up completely, or had never been here in the first place.

This part of the note was awfully scribbly. Maybe she'd rewritten it more neatly, then tossed this.

Yeah, right, because you care about pretty handwriting when you're scared and asking somebody to run away with you.

I went back to the computer. I stared at the theater's website. I clicked over and stared at my blank screenplay. There was only one way to put my mind at ease.

I need to talk to Megan.

❧

"Yes, Camille?" came Diana Brixton's tinny voice over the phone. "Did you get my package?"

"Yes, thank you! That manual will be really helpful. And it will be nice to see you at Thanksgiving." I cringed even as I said it; it sounded like I thought they were inviting me to join them. "I mean, to check in with you, and all—I'll be doing my own thing for the holiday, don't worry."

"Of course."

"So, I'm just calling because—well, I'm all settled in here in the guesthouse, but there were a few things I wanted to ask Megan. May I get her number from you?"

There was a brief pause, just a moment. "What things are those?"

"Oh, they aren't—I mean, it's nothing big. Just, little things that she could easily answer. I didn't want to bother you with them."

You're bothering me now, she didn't have to say. "You can just ask me. Since you have me on the line."

"Right, uh…" My mind flailed about wildly. "So, behind the guesthouse here, on the porch, there are a few pots of herbs and stuff, flowers. Growing things. I wondered if they were hers, if I should water them or something? Or if she's planning to come back for them?" *Jeez, Cam*, I thought. *You want to write an exciting screenplay and you can't invent something better than this? "Growing things?"*

Mrs. Brixton gave a soft *harrumph*. "I'm sure I don't know. Just go ahead and water them, or not, as it suits you. If they were important to her, she would have taken them."

"Right. But. Well."

"Was there anything else?"

"Yeah, well—you can't just give me her number?"

Now she sighed. "Camille, I would if I could, but I'm afraid I don't have it."

"You—what?"

"I told you that she left abruptly. She sent a registered letter, resigning effective immediately, for 'personal reasons.' Of course I phoned her the moment I received it. Her cell number had been disconnected, with no forwarding number."

"Oh."

Another almost imperceptible pause. "So you see, I'm afraid you'll have to use your own best judgment in dealing with the herbs and whatever other detritus Megan may have left behind. There is a tool shed at the back of the property; just pile anything in there that's in your way."

"Um, okay. Thank you, Mrs. Brixton. Sorry to bother you."

Her voice softened. "That's quite all right. We'll be in touch again soon."

I sat holding the phone for a long time after she hung up, just staring blankly at it.

Megan vanished.

Megan was frightened, wrote (and tore up) a desperate note, and then vanished.

Suddenly, this lovely, serene island seemed so much darker.

CHAPTER 4

I did what I could, but, being an even worse investigator than I was a screenplay writer, I didn't get very far.

The Washington State Ferry System representative I phoned was very sorry, but she could not share reservations records with me, or anyone, without a court order. So there was no way of knowing if Megan had shown up for her seven a.m. ferry last Thursday.

Anyway, I didn't even know her last name. Or what she drove.

I searched the guesthouse thoroughly for any more signs of her—the drawers in every room, the few books on the shelves, even flipping through her copy of the house manual. I found nothing. She may have left in a hurry, but she had taken all her clothes, all her toiletries, everything personal. The provisions in the kitchen were the only indication that anyone had lived here at all.

Well, the provisions, and the note in the fireplace.

Maybe I should ask Lisa Cannon what she knew about Megan. Sheila was one of her actors. Was Gregory?

How would Lisa feel about me prying into this? Deputy Rankin had basically told me that I had no idea how things worked out here on the island. Lisa had been very nice, but also a little—reserved? Underneath the friendliness? She'd acted like she hadn't even minded having the cops called on her, spending several hours getting that all sorted out yesterday. That had to have been a giant pain in the butt, never mind how "nice" it was to talk to Deputy Rankin.

Probably Lisa and Megan hadn't even met. Megan had only been here three weeks, after all.

I shivered again. A fire sounded like a good idea; it was growing chilly. I brought in a few logs from the back porch, then laid out newspaper and kindling.

The flames were crackling nicely. I was about to damp the flue down a little to send more heat into the room when I heard that strange bell. This time, at least, I knew what it was.

"Yes?" I said into the intercom.

"Camille?" A man's voice. My heart gave a frightened thump.

"Yes; who is this?"

"Colin. From down the road. Came to see what kind of casserole you like."

I was no longer afraid, but I was irritated. I did not want this. *Don't be nice to me!* I thought. *I'm an emotional basket case, I'm grieving and depressed and you don't want to come anywhere near me...*

But. I thought about my isolation, my resolution. *He's being neighborly,* I told myself sternly. *Nothing wrong with that.* "Come on down," I said, and pushed the button to open the gate. Steeling myself against his good looks, I went out and walked around to the front of the main house, meeting the familiar red pickup as it parked. Colin hopped down; I looked him over.

Yep. Just as stupidly gorgeous as before.

"Nice house," he said, gazing up at the mansion. "Haven't been here in a while—always forget how big it is."

"Too big for one person."

"For sure."

"The Brixtons are coming out for Thanksgiving anyway," I told him. "Where I'm living is more reasonable. And I've just built a fire." I led him around to the guest cottage. He wiped his boots on the mat and followed me in.

"Ah, that's more like it," he said, standing before the fire, warming his hands.

I sat in the easy chair closest to the fireplace, watching the flames pick up amber highlights in his dark curls. "You didn't come out here because you're wanting to bake me a casserole," I said.

He laughed. "No, but I'm willing to, if that's what it takes. Going back to the drinks idea."

"I—"

He held up a hand, stopping me. "Sorry. I should explain. Now, no offense to your charms and all, but I'm not exactly looking for anything myself. Similar reasons to yours." A flicker of grief crossed his face, just a moment of it, but it was enough to make me embarrassed about my assumptions. "But it occurs to me that, being new on the island and all, you don't know a soul here. Right?"

"Well, I did meet the next-door neighbor."

"Lisa Cannon. My mother used to say, butter wouldn't melt in her mouth. But she's not going to introduce you to anybody fun. I can." He flashed me his adorable grin. "So, I could bring you that casserole, and we could even eat it together, and at the end of the evening, you'd know one person. Or, I could take you to town, we could get a drink at the Barnacle, and at the end of the evening, you'd have met a dozen or more folks. What do you think?"

"I…" I stared at him helplessly. "I'm not much of a club person."

"A club? I don't know what Orcas would do with a club," he said with a chuckle. "Barnacle's just a little local spot. Something to drink, some eats. I'm just looking to get out a little. Nothing more, Cam, I'm not ready." His eyes were honest, and warm, and…mesmerizing. And what did I have here? Mysteries, wor-

ries, grief, that stupid blank screen where a screenplay was supposed to be. And all that baby bok choy.

"All right. The Barnacle it is."

❧

I insisted on following his truck in my Honda, because that's
what you do when you're being careful: you take your own car.
My precautions felt a little…big-city-ish. Well, what could I say?
I was a big-city girl. I'd been here three days. Island life would
take a little getting used to.

We drove up Prune Alley in Eastsound, past the question-
able-looking Lower Tavern, past the grocery store. We just…
parked. No circling the block, no meter, no cursing. Just parking.

"Wow…" I sighed, as we stood in the doorway. The Barnacle
was tiny, crowded, and just precious. The entire place was one
room the size of a boathouse. Rows of colored bottles lined the
windows up to the peaked-roof ceiling. The bar itself was con-
structed out of a single enormous piece of polished driftwood.
The plush, comfy-looking bar stools were all taken, but by some
native-islander magic, Colin snagged a small two-person table
near the front door.

"What do you think?" he asked with a grin, handing me a
cocktail menu.

I squinted, trying to read in the dim light. "It's amazing. And
a little packed!"

"Only open weekends during the winter, so we make the most
of it."

There's a lot of 'making the most of things' during the winter, I
thought.

The bartender was standing over us, casually but neatly dressed,
her hair pulled back in a loose bun. "Hey," she said to Colin, and
then to me: "What'll it be?"

I glanced up at her, then back to the menu. "I'm thinking the
Vesper Twist, is that good?"

She grinned. "The best." Then she turned to Colin. "And you, big boy?"

"The usual, Miss Darling."

"Right-o." As she turned to go, a small red curl escaped her bun.

"Oh!" I said, before I could stop myself. "You're the FedEx Lady!"

She turned back around and smiled even wider. "That's my day job; now I'm Bartender Chick. And you're the Brixton Caretaker Gal."

"I am."

"Welcome to the island. I'll get your drinks, and then we'll chat."

She was back in a minute with two glasses, but just left them on the table with a nod and a smile as she darted back to the bar. It hadn't seemed possible, but the place was even more crowded now; people were lined two and three deep at the bar, all the tables were filled, and a few folks even stood outside, cold as it was. Or maybe they were smokers. FedEx Lady, I mean Bartender Chick, bustled about, that same easy grin on her face, taking care of everyone.

"She's good," I said to Colin, then took a sip of my drink. "Ooh, this is good too." Bright and citrusy, but plenty of gin. Yum.

He smiled back at me and swigged his beer. "Yeah, Jen's great."

"Jen?"

He nodded. "Jen Darling."

"Oh! I thought that was just an endearment. I was wondering, since you're not ready and all." And where was this sudden feeling of relief coming from? *You are* not *looking for romance. You are* not.

His eyes glinted in the low light. "She's everyone's darling, in more ways than one. I grew up with her—she's another native. Fewer of us around all the time, it seems." He glanced around the room, and turned back to me with a sheepish shrug. "I know I said I'd be able to introduce you to dozens of people, but I hardly know anyone here."

"Do most people move away?"

"Yeah. It's hard enough, growing up out here on the edge of the ocean, the edge of everything, you know? But we get flooded with tourists every summer, and it's like, you can't even live in your own space. It belongs to a bunch of rich strangers."

It was the longest he'd talked, yet.

I glanced around at the crowded bar as well. "It seems really comfortable right now." We were surrounded by people of all ages, having a great time with each other.

"Winters are the best. Despite the weather." Colin took another sip of his beer. "Talking about the weather! Must be charming the heck out of you."

I laughed too. "I actually find weather *fascinating*. Do tell me more."

"Just wait till one of the big storms rolls in. You'll find plenty to get fascinated with—trees down on the road, floods in your basement, leaky roof… "

"You think the Brixton place is going to spring some leaks?"

He chuckled. "Okay, maybe not. It's like Noah's ark. It'll float."

"You guys gonna eat, or just drink?" Jen Darling was back standing over us.

I shrugged, and looked at Colin, who shrugged back. "Just drink for now, I guess."

"Okay!" And she was gone again, wiping down a table for a new group to sit at, memorizing their orders without writing anything down.

I didn't know if it was the drink (delicious) or the low light or the laid-back atmosphere, but I was finding myself less irritated by Colin's good looks. Maybe it was like looking at the sun, and I was going blind. But he no longer seemed so dazzling. He just seemed like…a guy.

"So," I said to Colin, "you do boat repair in the winter and boat tours during the summer. Do you live on a boat?"

I'd been half-joking, but he said, "Yeah. At least for now. Got a sweet little thirty-three-foot sloop down in the West Sound harbor. Happy to show you around some day, even take you on a little sail if you like."

I surprised myself with my answer. "I'd like that."

"Great."

The thought of boating unfortunately brought back the memory of the fellow motoring in to the little bay my first morning. I shoved it away at once. I was through with manufacturing Orcas intrigue. "What's that like, living on your boat?"

"Cozy."

I nodded. "How about when one of those storms rolls in?"

He laughed and shook his head at the same time. "Not pretty! But she's tight; never had a problem."

I had nothing else to say about boats. I took a sip of my drink to stall for time. "That's good," I finally said instead. "Listen," I blurted. "I'm terrible with small talk. I hate it."

"Well," he said, "I could ask you real questions."

"I…think I'd prefer real questions. Though I reserve the right not to answer."

He nodded. "That's fair. You don't like a question, just turn it around on me."

"All right." I smiled at him, my heart beating fast. But my skin was calm. That was something, anyway.

"So, tell me about that last relationship, and why it ended."

I leaned back a bit. "You go straight to the heart of things, don't you?"

He grinned and gave another shrug. "You did want *real* questions. But you don't have to tell me. It's all good."

"No, I do want to tell you—" *At least some of it*, I added silently. "It's good to talk about it." I paused, gathering my thoughts. "His name was Kevin. I mean, is Kevin. He's still alive and he hasn't changed it. So far as I know."

Colin had the good grace to smile at my lame humor. That's what it was: humor. Not just babbling.

I cleared my throat and continued. "We were together about a year and a half, but only living together for the last few months. He's a good guy, but maybe a little insecure. He always…I don't know, wanted to be closer than I was ready for. But he was pretty good about that. Most of the time, anyway." I fell silent again, thinking. How to tell it? I couldn't explain about the vanishing; if I'd learned one thing in the Kevin-disaster, it was to keep that to myself, always and forever.

"Did he push you?" Colin prompted, when I'd been quiet for too long.

"Well, yes and no. He was always on me to let him in further, to trust him, to open myself to him. And I did—I mean, I tried. But there's a core of me that's just…different from other people. Something he was never going to understand. And that bothered him. I tried to explain…I told him I'd shared more with him than anyone else, ever, which was true; but somehow, that was never quite good enough. He just kept trying for that last, elusive piece."

Colin was looking at me seriously, listening hard. Trying to understand, despite my necessarily vague words. "Sounds like a lot of pressure."

"Yeah. It was." I sighed, taking another sip of my drink. Probably time to order another. "I thought things had gotten better. He'd stopped pressing; we were doing really well. I'd moved in, and that was good too. It was my birthday. He'd been hinting about having some nice surprise planned…I was actually thinking he might be going to propose." I bit my lip. It sounded so stupid, so pathetic. "And then…well, that isn't what happened. Instead we had the worst fight we'd ever had, and…he stormed out, said we were through.

"I had just been talking with a client that afternoon—Mrs.

Brixton. She'd been desperate, their last caretaker had up and quit with no notice, after all the trouble she'd gone to find and train her, and she didn't know what she was going to do. So, before Kevin could even come back to the apartment, I called her. She said come on over, so I threw a bunch of stuff in my car and—well, here I am." I gave him a shy smile. "Now do I get to ask you a hard question? I mean a *real* question?"

He smiled back. "Seems fair."

"All right." I watched his lovely dark eyes. "What about you? You said you had a similar situation to me. Or do you just make a practice of introducing newcomers to the island?"

Colin laughed. "Believe it or not, this is my first time doing that. Not even sure why I pulled over to talk to you. Something…just drew me." He shrugged. "But to your question: I was with a woman who grew up here as well. Beth. Together almost fifteen years. You find that here, with the locals. Childhood sweethearts who grow up and stay together for decades. Maybe even their whole lives. I thought that was us, to be honest. We never married but I didn't think we had to. I don't know, maybe we should have. Toward the end, we grew so far apart, we were like roommates. Finally, she left the island. She'd always wanted to live somewhere bigger, more exciting."

"Where did she go?"

"Omaha."

I burst out laughing; Colin laughed with me. "I know, I know," he went on. "I mean, it is bigger; but what really happened is she got a job there that she couldn't pass up. She still hopes to get to New York, or at least Boston or Philly or someplace like that." He looked wistful. "We're still in touch, still friends. Or trying to be. You know."

I didn't. I tended to go and stay gone. Remaining friends wasn't part of my vocabulary. "Did you live on your boat together?"

"Nah, we had a house. Couldn't afford it alone."

Jen Darling came back over. "Another round?"

"Yeah," Colin said, and then glanced at me. I nodded. "And maybe the cheese board?"

"Comin' right up."

"The boat's a little tight for two," Colin continued. "Cozy for one. I won't live there forever; hadn't even planned to live there this long, but there's been no real reason to leave it. So." He grinned again. Something about his relaxed, friendly manner, along with his openness and honesty—his lack of interest in small talk and games—he was great to talk to.

"My turn to ask another one," he said, with a wicked sparkle in his eye.

"Oh gosh, look at the time," I joked, looking at my empty wrist. I'd left my watch at the house. Like you do when you go clubbing.

He laughed. "No, this one will be easy. Do you like to hike?"

"Hike?"

"You know, muddy trails, amazing views, protein bars for lunch."

I smiled back at him. "Yes, in fact, I love to hike. Or walk in general. I like being outdoors."

"Well, you've come to the right place. I can show you—"

Bartender Jen returned with our drinks and a gorgeous little platter of cheeses and other nibbles. This time, she pulled up a chair and sat with us; the bar was a lot less crowded, I suddenly noticed. "Dig in," she said. "I'm just gonna bother you two on your date, don't mind me."

"It's not a date." I was quiet but firm.

"Are you sure about that?" Jen was smiling.

Colin shrugged. "Struck out again."

Jen just laughed. "Just your luck, Colin," she said, then turned to me. "Try the chevre, it's amazing."

Now that the food was in front of me, I realized I was starving. "Wow, yes," I said, around a mouthful. "That's incredible."

"So, what do you do when you're not being Caretaker Gal?"

she asked.

"I'm writing a screenplay," I said around another mouthful. "About a hairdresser."

"Oh good," Jen sighed with theatrical relief. "You're a two-jobber, like the rest of us *real* people. Now we can be friends—I was hoping we could."

"Two-jobber?"

"Everyone on Orcas is either a two-jobber—or more—or a no-jobber. You know: retired surgeons and tech-industry folks, living on their vast fortunes."

I thought about gracious, well-groomed Lisa Cannon. And, heck, the Brixtons. No-jobbers *and* two-housers. "Ah. Of course."

"The two-jobbers are the ones who run the island—waitressing, bartending, working at the grocery store, delivering packages. The no-jobbers *own* the island."

I took another bite of cheese. "I'm not sure you can call my screenwriting a job. I've never gotten paid for writing anything." I paused. "I've never actually really finished writing anything, if you want to know the truth."

Jen and Colin both laughed. "Gotta start somewhere," he said, as she nodded.

The door opened, and a group of four came in. "Oops, back to work," Jen said, popping to her feet and greeting the newcomers with a warm smile.

"Don't know any of them, either," Colin said, frowning as the group took their places at the bar. "I feel like a stranger on my own island."

"Well, you know me, at least a little," I said, smiling at him.

He grinned back at me. "Yes. That takes away some of the sting."

I burst out laughing again, then looked down at the cheese board while I tried to remember what I hadn't liked about this guy when I met him outside that empty restaurant. His looks? His gruff speech? Or was it just having a man I didn't know approach me? It could have been anything, but my initial impression was completely off base. He was a nice guy.

"Thanks for getting me out of the house," I said at last. "This has been really fun."

"My pleasure. Didn't get you a crowd, but at least you know two people now."

❧

At the end of the evening, there was no post-date awkwardness as he saw me to my car, since we hadn't been on a date. We'd gotten along so well, so comfortably. I should have let him give me a ride after all. "Hey, at least you don't have to drive all the way back out to the Brixtons'," I said, feeling a little guilty.

"True that."

I followed his truck back to West Sound, turning right when he turned left to go to the harbor, where he lived. On a boat. Living on a boat! That sounded so exotic to me. "Cozy," he'd called it. I smiled, letting myself back into my chilly guesthouse. The fire, of course, had completely died by this point. But it was after eleven; too late to light another. Might as well just tuck myself into bed. Tomorrow would be here all too soon.

It was so nice to have taken an entire evening off from mysteries and worries, I realized. I could have asked Colin or Jen about Lisa Cannon, about her theater company, about this mysterious Sheila. Even about Megan—whether either of them had met her during her few short weeks here. Instead, I'd relaxed and drank lovely cocktails and eaten delicious cheese. And, yes, Colin was right: I'd gotten to know a couple of very nice people.

I had lived for twenty-seven years with my pains and my history and my secrets. In city after city, blending in and hiding in plain sight, leaving when things got uncomfortable. I'd shut people out for most of my life, and I was ready to start letting them in. Was this beautiful little island the place it could happen?

It took a long time to fall asleep.

CHAPTER 5

Five a.m. came as early as it ever did. After fighting it a while, I gave up, got out of bed, and poked around with my screenplay for a few hours. I was able to focus better today, managing to create the major characters, describe the setting, and even get a scene started.

What was I writing? It had started out as something of a mystery, with an elderly (but still quite spry) client who didn't show up to an appointment she kept religiously, setting off the stylist's alarm bells. There was some low-grade investigation at the client's home, and a suspiciously over-involved nephew who stood to inherit a lot of money. But then an attractive investigating officer arrived. It was starting to get a little meet-cute romantic comedy.

At least it was something.

I actually felt pretty good about my efforts by lunchtime. No doubt that would completely evaporate over the course of the day, but I stood up and stretched, feeling like I had something to show for my exertions. I wandered through the little house. I'd take a break, maybe go for a walk, and see if I could finish the scene in the afternoon.

But first, a turkey sandwich on white bread. I thought, as I ate it, that Kevin would have *hated* it, earnest foodie that he was. I felt a pang, and my heart caught up in my throat, remembering his tall, skinny frame suspended over the artisan breads at the Pike Place Market, trying to choose the perfect loaf. Smiling, flipping his dreadlocks out of his green eyes.

This one has a fantastic crumb.

I hadn't cried yet this day. I refused to start. I opened the front door to have a glance at the weather—cloudy, but no rain in the immediate future—and pulled on my hiking boots and jacket. I'd already gone up Deer Harbor Road to the West Sound harbor; this time, I'd go the opposite direction, try to make Deer Harbor itself.

Of course, that meant going past the Cannon estate. The gates were shut as I walked past; I peered through the trees, but saw no signs of life.

Deer Harbor turned out to be closer than West Sound harbor; I was there in fifteen minutes or so. I walked around a bit, but it didn't have a whole lot to offer. It looked to be much more of a working marina than a tourist one, though there was a little store here, and it even had an espresso counter. I strode right in and ordered a cappuccino from the teenaged barista.

"We only have whole milk," he said, looking worried.

"That's okay." Did I look that much in need of skim?

Despite the rich milk, the coffee itself was a little thin. Brown Bear Bakery made much better caffeine-bearing elixir. This place would serve in a caffeine emergency. Always good to have a back-up.

Licking foam off my top lip, I dropped a dollar in the tip jar, just like a person who could afford to do that. I almost convinced myself. I went back out to the road, intending to explore further. Just past the marina, though, the road curved sharply up away from the water, leading to a development of newish-looking smaller houses. Not very inviting, or interesting.

Well, this was a good enough walk.

I turned around and started back home, already thinking about the rest of my opening scene. I wanted to get the action going right away. So something weird or upsetting or dramatic had to happen pretty quickly. Above and beyond the disappearance, or non-appearance, of the elderly client, of course, and the vague sliminess of her nephew. What weirdness could possibly happen in a hair salon?

Actually, the more I thought about it, the more ideas I had. The nephew's girlfriend, of course, should also be a client. No, wait—*ex*-girlfriend. Yeah. And she should have things she wanted to tell the main character, though not here in the salon; she should insist on meeting for drinks downtown... No, at a sleazy nightclub at midnight...

I was lost in my imagined scene, not paying much attention to the world around me, when I suddenly realized I was almost back to the Brixtons'. In fact I was right in front of Lisa Cannon's place. The gates were now standing open. I peered down the driveway. There were two cars parked in front of her freakishly large garage: what looked like a Bentley or some other luxury vehicle, and a plain, smaller sedan—some kind of Toyota, I thought.

As I was watching, the driver's door of the Toyota opened, and Sheila stepped out.

My heart started pounding with fear, and I felt my skin give its telltale tingle. I tried breathing more slowly and regularly—sometimes that helped—as I told myself, *You're up here on a public road. She can't hurt you. She didn't even kill that guy, anyway.*

So why was Megan afraid of her? Because even after what I'd seen, Sheila didn't look particularly frightening. She looked like a thickset woman of middle age with a sad lack of physical charms. Awkward, but not scary. The kind of earnest, well-meaning person who rescues pit bulls.

Megan didn't say she was afraid of Sheila. She was scared, and she talked to Sheila, and then the note was torn off. Probably she was friends *with Sheila.*

I watched Sheila retrieve market bags from the backseat.

Just go talk to her, I told myself. Clearly she knew Megan; if there were something wrong, maybe she'd know more information. Maybe she had Megan's new contact information. *Just ask her some questions, put your mind at ease.* My skin was still tingling—like pins and needles, but more gently. While I stood on the road dithering, Sheila unloaded even more bags from the trunk of the car. She'd grabbed too many at a time, the plastic handles digging into her fingers. I could almost feel the lack of circulation in my own fingers as she carried them past the main entrance and around the side of the house. I heard the jingle of keys. Opening a side door?

You're scared of an actor coming home with groceries? I chided myself furiously. Wishing I was more brave. Wishing I was less broken. *Just go talk to her. Apologize for turning her in, put things right between you. She will probably laugh, Cam, because it is absurd, right?*

Get this out of your system before you panic fully.

That coffee might have been weak, but it and fear had gotten my heart hammering. I took a few deep breaths, looked at the sun, the sky, the peaceful trees and the completely unthreatening cars. It was too early in the day for a glass of wine, but I wished like heck I had one to calm my skin. After a long moment, my heart began to slow, and my skin settled. I started walking down Lisa Cannon's driveway, breathing deeply. Before I got to the Toyota, I heard a door close.

Well, crap. I'd missed her.

(Oh thank goodness.)

Turning back to head home, I heard, "Camille!" It was Lisa, hailing me from the front door.

"Oh hi!" I said, flushing with embarrassment as I walked back toward her. "I'm sorry—I was just out for a walk, I thought I saw…" Well, what did I think I saw? I had no idea how to explain why I was wandering around in her driveway.

But she just smiled. "Another murder?" I erupted in laughter and she gave a tinkling laugh in response. Laughter settled my skin completely. "No, I guess not; no rehearsals today. Sorry that we're not more interesting neighbors. Have you had lunch?"

"I did, yes; I was about to get back to writing. I'm sorry to bother you. I was just…in the neighborhood. I should have called, I guess."

"No, not at all! We don't do that here, Camille. We don't call first, we just drop by. Come on in for a minute; I've just made a pot of hot chocolate."

"Well…okay, that actually sounds really good."

Soon we were seated—just the two of us—in her plush living room, this time with cups of thick, rich hot chocolate. *Very* thick. "This is almost like pudding," I said.

Lisa smiled. "It's called sipping chocolate. I get it in Eastsound, at Kathryn Taylor. They don't sell it to the general public, but she makes an exception for me." She gave an abashed little smile as she touched her cup to her lips. "I'm a terrible addict."

Kathryn Taylor. I'd heard of their chocolates; Kevin had had some in a restaurant once and then hunted them down online, had talked about ordering some. Again, my heart sank. I smiled weakly back at Lisa, trying not to think about what might be involved in convincing a boutique chocolate purveyor to make something special just for you, just because you really like it. Because you want it.

And a winery too, come to think of it. Did Lisa buy anything that the rest of us did?

Heck, I was lucky to live next door to her—at least she was generous with her exquisite spoils. "I didn't see a murder," I said, answering her question so belatedly, she was probably confused. Would I *ever* learn how to make small talk? "I just saw your actor come in with some bags. I was going to offer to help, and apologize for calling the police on her, but then she was gone."

"My actor?" Lisa looked confused a moment, then nodded. "Oh, Sheila, of course. Yes. Well, Sheila isn't actually an actor. Though she helps with running lines." She called back over her shoulder. "Sheila? Sheila, are you around?" Lisa looked back with a reassuring smile. "You two really should meet, don't you think?"

"Yeah?" Sheila thumped into the room, solemn-faced, and stopped short when she saw me. Or maybe it was the rug that brought her up short. She stood beside it, not on it, keeping her dusty boots away from its beauty.

Lisa, ever gracious, made introductions. "Sheila, this is our new neighbor, Cam. She's taking care of the Brixton place these days."

"Oh." Sheila looked down at her boots, then back up with a scowl. "Do you know where Megan went? She left something here and I don't know what to do with it."

My pins-and-needles were faint, but still there. "I'm sorry, I don't. In fact I'd been wondering if either of you might have any idea where she was."

"I'm afraid I don't," said Lisa. "Sheila? Any information about Megan's whereabouts?"

Sheila scratched the top of her head, then shook it. "Not even a little."

Lisa shook her head as well, and smiled at Sheila. "Do you want to join us for some sipping chocolate?"

"Yuck, no." Sheila crossed her arms. "I don't want any of that goopy stuff. I like Swiss Miss. What's wrong with Swiss Miss?"

Lisa smiled. "Is all the provender put away, or can we come help?"

Sheila actually looked offended. "I can handle it myself." Without another word, she clumped off to some far corner of this vast and elegant home.

"I obviously didn't hire Sheila for her manners. But trust me, under that gruff façade, she has a heart a mile wide. And a real fondness for Swiss Miss instant cocoa." Lisa gave me a brilliant smile and then leaned forward, setting her cup on the table. "How is the writing going?"

"Good, but slowly," I said. "At this rate, I'll have a full-length screenplay in, oh, two or three years?" I smiled to show I was joking, but Lisa nodded seriously.

"Are you sure it's a screenplay, and not a stage play? I mean, have you considered the stage as a venue? We're always looking for new material, and a play about the quirky people a hairdresser encounters sounds very entertaining."

I frowned. "I'd imagined it as a movie, but I guess it could just as easily be a play."

"It doesn't have to be one or the other. Plays get made into movies all the time."

"Right." I thought about it. "The setting might be complicated—it doesn't just take place in the hair salon. It moves around, all over the city, as Felicia—the main character—follows clues and solves the mystery."

Lisa waved away this objection. "Setting is no problem. We can do plenty with props and lighting and special effects, never mind the actual scenery. How many characters are you planning?"

"Three main characters, plus a lot of minor ones."

"The play we're rehearsing right now has thirteen parts, but only two actors—plenty of characters is no barrier either. I'll get you a ticket when it opens, you should come. Cam, I'm serious: your salon confessional sounds really intriguing. As soon as you finish a few scenes, let me see them."

I was starting to get a little excited despite myself. Here I had barely started my play, I mean screenplay, and already a well-heeled producer was interested in it! Okay, in a very small market, but even so. "All right," I said, trying to hide my smile.

Lisa Cannon was good at drawing me out, I decided. I'd never talked about my screenplay with anyone, not even with Kevin, and here she'd pulled it all out of me. She leaned back, still smiling. "I'm so glad to have you next door. Listen: I do a sort of casual happy hour gathering over here most weeknights, especially during rehearsals. Whoever is around just drops in. I'd be so pleased if you would join us—whenever you're free."

I opened my mouth to decline, what with all the things I had to do, like writing, watering plants, eating baby bok choy. "Um, sure, that sounds great. What can I bring?"

She shrugged. "You don't need to bring anything. I just set out a variety of wines and maybe some little nibbles. Folks come and go. Completely casual."

"I'd love to." I couldn't believe this was me talking. I was reserved and wary and I stayed away from people I didn't know. But there was something about this island, the smallness of it, the charm.

And my increasing thought that perhaps things could be different here.

Lisa finished her little cup of chocolate delight and set the cup on its saucer with a gentle but definitive clink. I finished mine as well and got to my feet.

"I hope to see you again later," Lisa said, walking me to the door. "Things generally get started around five-thirty. Oh, and no need to climb back up to the road—there's a path between our places, just past where the fence stops." She pointed to the little patch of woods that separated the houses. "Shouldn't be too muddy at the moment. Straight through there, and you'll be home in a minute."

"Thanks!"

I started through the woods, finding the path easily. I was most of the way through when I realized that this was just where I had seen Sheila and Gregory rehearsing that first morning. The thought gave me the shivers; I could see the gunshot, and him falling, all over again. Sheila might not be an actor, but she'd been convincing.

Well, she did have that gruff manner to her.

I slowed down, looking at the ground as I went by. Here: yes, it had been right here. It had rained a bit since then, but not much; I saw a vague imprint on the ground where Gregory had fallen. I stopped and bent down, looking more closely. Not only was there the impression of a body; there were also long scrapes in the dirt leading away from it. Signs of a body being dragged?

How far had they taken this scene they were rehearsing?

What play, exactly, *were* they rehearsing? Not *Murder for Two*. Why hadn't I asked about that? I would, when I came back for happy hour. I totally would. I could play off like it was the curiosity of a playwright. Showing interest in the process and all.

I stood back up, still staring at the ground, frowning. It was just peculiar, is what it was.

Was this why Lisa was being so nice to me? So I wouldn't poke around in her business?

But everyone was so nice here. It was a nice island, full of nice people, just spending all day being nice. Me and my big-city paranoia. Lisa had sent me home this way, after all. She wasn't hiding anything. She had just invited me to come back any time I wanted—to just drop in. That wasn't what people did if they were trying to hide something.

A sound behind me made me startle; footsteps, the crunch of a boot on dead leaves. I took a quick breath in and turned.

It was Sheila, stomping straight up the path toward me, looking as grim as she had on that first morning. Was she looking for me?

Moving just as mechanically as I had the first day, forgetting entirely that I'd just met her and she was harmless, I took a quiet step off the path and behind a tree. My skin flamed into action; my veins hammered; my voice vanished. I was invisible.

I looked down at myself, stunned that I'd gone there so fast, so unthinkingly.

When I chameleon, it's not like I literally disappear; that's impossible, of course, and anyway my clothes would give me away. It's more like, there's an aura that comes around me, a layer of… deflection. I blend in. It's hard to look at me, even for myself; it's nearly impossible to see me. I vanish.

No matter what my logical mind was trying to tell me, my body had decided to go full chameleon.

Sheila walked down the path right by me. She wouldn't be able to see me, but she would hear my footsteps if I tried to step around her—presuming I wasn't still frozen. She might even sense my presence; a lifetime of dealing with this affliction had taught me that that was much worse. The only thing for it was to stay in the shadows until I became visible again, and then ease back into sight in some natural-seeming way, if I couldn't avoid contact altogether.

Sheila stopped just past my tree, staring forward. Then she turned to gaze behind her.

"What is it?" Lisa called from the house.

"Nothing. I thought I saw something," Sheila called back. I could have reached out and touched her arm; I focused on keeping my breathing as quiet as possible.

"It's just the neighbor," Lisa called. "Cam. She took the short-cut."

Sheila gave a snort. "Then she's fast." I could smell the instant cocoa on her breath, she was that close. Could she smell my sipping chocolate? "I just wanted to be sure—" she started.

"Leave it; come back to the house." Lisa's voice was commanding and short; there was none of the easy, relaxed warmth she had shown me. "We need to get all this put away."

"Sure thing, boss lady." Sheila gazed down the path a moment longer, then turned and stomped back to the Cannon estate.

I stood in the shadows a while longer, breathing and letting my skin return to normal, making sure both women were safely inside. Getting control of my muscles again.

I threaded my way through the woods to the guesthouse, where I found the largest zucchini I'd ever seen leaning against my front door. I picked it up, unaccountably furious.

"Who keeps LEAVING THINGS HERE?"

I carried the thing into the house and set it on the counter, trembling. I was surprised to find myself on the verge of tears.

Had I ever really thought I could escape myself?

No, not seriously; my unwanted power would always be with me, wherever I went. But I had thought…I don't know what I'd thought. That I could move to a place where I didn't feel frightened, or threatened. That if I lived peacefully and remotely, I could stay placid enough to remain—visibly—in my own skin.

That somehow, some day, the nightmares might stop.

I shook my head and went to the sink for a glass of water. "There is nobody being murdered next door!" I said aloud to my reflection in the kitchen window. "The only drama around here is on your computer screen. Which you should be getting back to, missy."

Yes, ma'am, I thought, and went back to work.

❧

The lovely flow I'd had all morning was nowhere to be found. In fact I ended up erasing two-thirds of what I'd written, then going back to my path of pacing through the little house, looking for inspiration.

I'd made four or five laps when my cell phone rang, catching me in a patch of coverage. I pulled the phone out of my pocket, and cringed. "Mom," I said, after I'd swiped to accept the call.

Lauren Jonas was not my birth mom, but she was the closest thing I had in my life after the age of four. I did remember my real mom…though most of what I remembered was so embedded in tragedy, I tried not to think about her often.

"Camille Tate, where in the world are you?"

I straightened my shoulders and took a deep breath. "Orcas Island. In the San Juans. Kevin and I split up, and I had to leave."

"But your job!"

"I got a new job—I'm being paid very well to caretake a gorgeous estate, right on the water. Way more than I was making at the salon. And our chair fees were about to go up anyway."

"But you didn't tell me any of this!"

And there it was. I sighed. "I'm sorry, Mom. It all happened very, very fast. I've only been here a couple of days; I'm still just getting settled in." I added, before she could object further, "It's amazing here. You and Dad should come out and visit!" Was I allowed to have guests here? This cottage did have an extra bedroom...

"What about Thanksgiving? I thought you were coming home. Cliff's still in Thailand. You *have* to come home."

"I...don't think I can leave so soon. Hey—why don't you come out here for the holiday?"

"What?"

"Yeah, let me check with the owners; they're coming out for Thanksgiving. I'll see if you can stay here with me—I have my own little house on the grounds. Though it's only little in comparison to theirs—it has plenty of room."

She gave a heavy sigh. "Well, I haven't ordered the turkey yet..."

Wait, she was actually considering it? I was momentarily stunned. But it would be really nice to have my foster parents out here. They would love the island. "Yes, talk to Dad, and I'll call the owners."

"Oh, I don't know." Now she was backpedaling. If I pushed, she'd retreat further.

"Just think about it," I said quickly. "You don't have to decide now. We have some time."

"All right." She was silent a moment. "What in the world happened with Kevin? I thought you two were so happy together. I thought he was the one."

I sighed again. "I thought so too. But, the more I think about it, the more I realize that things had been difficult for a while."

"Living together is a big step..."

I was pacing through the house again by now, peering into the guest room, thinking about what I would need to do to make it up for company. "Yeah. He really wanted to; I thought it would... Well. It was probably too soon."

"When it's right, you know."

I sighed. "Kevin thought it was right. I wanted it to be right. But then—well, we had a fight, and he walked out. And I just realized that I had to go, and fast. If I'd waited for him to come home, I might have…given too much away. You know. I didn't want to do that any more. I just knew I was done."

"Oh, honey."

"I'm all right, really. I mean, I'm sad, but…it gets a little better every day."

"You certainly put a good face on it. I had no idea."

"Yeah. I'm good at that."

Her voice softened. "Yes, my dear. You are too quiet for your own good. I'm sorry you're going through this. It must be hard." She phrased the last sentence as almost a question—an invitation to talk about it further, but not a demand.

"It is hard. And I'm sorry I didn't tell you. I'm working on getting better about that sort of thing."

"I forgive you, honey." She paused, then added, "Have you given any more thought to therapy?"

"No." How could I work with a therapist if I couldn't reveal my secrets?

"Well, if you ever change your mind…I'm sure I could find the name of someone good. Listen, I have to go, but don't disappear again without telling me, please? I don't like it when you vanish on me."

"I know, Mom. I hate vanishing, too." I cringed again at the word choice, shook my head. If she only knew. "I'm sorry. Let's talk in a few days, okay?"

"Yes. I'll call you again."

I hesitated, but only for a moment. *Don't push on Thanksgiving. Let her decide.* "I love you."

"I love you too."

After we'd hung up, I dialed Diana Brixton, bracing myself for her prickly why-are-you-bothering-me-yet-again attitude.

"Hello, Camille!" she cried instead. "How are things?"

"Um, fine. Listen, I'm sorry to bother you—"

"You're not a bother! You're taking care of our precious house! Everything is fine, I hope?"

"Uh, yeah, it's all great." *Well, except for the bizarre mystery of your last caretaker.* "But I was wondering, I was just talking to my mom, and, well, I realized I never asked what your rules are for my having guests. I mean, here in the guesthouse."

"It is entirely permissible for you to have guests! When is she visiting?"

"Well, it'd be my mom and my dad, over Thanksgiving. Maybe—they haven't decided yet. Now, I know you guys are going to be here then too—"

"The more the merrier!" This was kind of weirding me out, to be perfectly honest. Was she drunk? In the middle of the afternoon? "We will be delighted to meet your parents! Perhaps we should all have dessert together while they're on the island."

"Sure, that would be great."

"We just have a few conditions for guests," she said, still bubbling over with suspicious cheer. "It's all covered in the house manual—in the second appendix, if you haven't found it already—but the basics are pretty simple. We just need a photocopy of the driver's licenses for every visitor, including their current home address; a copy of the registration for any car that will be on the grounds; and home and cell phone numbers for them all. And we'll need to know which ferries they will be taking, both coming and going."

"Um." *Seriously?* I thought. *I really need to look more carefully at this house manual.*

"Since they're your parents, I'll waive the usual requirement for letters of reference."

"*What?*"

She laughed. "Yes, Emmett and I have certainly learned a few lessons over the years!"

"Well, um, okay."

"Was there anything else?"

"No, that's all." I shook my head. "Thank you."

"Thank *you!*" She hung up.

I set the cell phone down on the kitchen counter and studied the enormous zucchini. Weird, too weird. The vegetable *and* the phone call. Well, it was nearly four; it was possible Mrs. Brixton had been drinking. If she'd started at lunch, and hadn't stopped, that might account for her peculiar cheerfulness.

At least she'd said yes. That was something.

Now thoroughly distracted from my screenplay, I headed back into the guest bedroom to see about making it ready for company. It was a nice room, of course; a bit smaller than the master bedroom, but still way bigger than the closet I'd repurposed as a guest bed in my Seattle apartment. Yes, my folks would be more than comfortable here.

Too bad that Cliff was so far away. I missed my foster brother.

The bed was not made up, but two blankets were folded neatly and piled at the foot, next to two down pillows. I opened the closet, looking for sheets, and found a nice flowered set with lace ruffles. I pulled them out and sniffed them: they smelled freshly laundered, not stale or musty. Maybe Megan had had guests; or maybe whoever was the caretaker before her did.

I began making up the bed, lifting the edges of the mattress to tuck the sheets in tightly, like Mom preferred. My fingers touched something under the upper left-hand corner. I stopped, lifting the mattress higher, looking. Blue, small, rectangular.

I reached in and pulled out a passport.

"Oh…" I sighed, sitting down on the bed to open it.

Yes, it was Megan's passport. I studied her face in the photo. She was blond, with delicate and pronounced bone structure, and she was twenty-five on her most recent birthday. Her last name was Duquesne. She'd gotten the passport four years ago, before a trip to Canada. Her permanent address was in Oregon.

I stood up and lifted the mattress all the way, sliding it to the floor. But there was nothing else underneath it.

I leafed through the passport again. From the timing, it looked like she'd taken a spring break trip to Mexico last year, and a few summertime runs up to Canada before that.

She would have never willingly left her passport behind. No one does that. What could this mean?

You know what it means.

Someone had carefully, thoroughly removed all of Megan Duquesne's belongings...but whoever that had been, it wasn't Megan.

CHAPTER 6

My night held more nightmares than sleep.

I honestly didn't know what to do. Should I follow the path of my imaginings to the point where I completely panicked and quit? Should I leave the island, forget any of this had ever happened? Was that what had happened to Megan?

I lay in the darkness that lingered too long before dawn, trying to figure it out.

I needed the money, and I needed the place to live—I'd given up my chair at the salon and of course my (well, Kevin's) apartment in Seattle. Those bridges were well and truly burnt. I could go stay with my folks for a week or two…but no, I didn't belong there, they didn't really have room for me; and I was twenty-seven years old, for crying out loud.

I should really have had my act better together by now.

I had come to at least a partial decision: I would take the passport to the sheriff's office, tell them what I'd seen and what I'd surmised about it, and leave it in their hands. Deputy Rankin had seemed nice enough. I wouldn't call 911 again; he would have to be pleased about that.

Then I would get on with island life. Caretake the heck out of this beautiful place. Write the dang screenplay. Stay away from creepy mysteries and enjoy my life.

I was finishing breakfast when my cell phone rang: Colin. Had I put his number in there, and his name? I must have, there it was. "Hey," I said.

"You sound excited for your big hiking day."

"Is that today?" I didn't remember setting a firm date. Had I?

"Not gonna get better weather than this for another week at least. Tomorrow the rain comes back."

I peered out the window: barely a cloud in the sky. A great day for hiking, but I didn't want to. What if Megan was in trouble? No, she wasn't in trouble. She'd hidden her passport for safety, and forgotten where she left it. People do that. I had done that. Well, not with my passport, but still. With other things, for sure.

I was going to be calm. I was going to give up these paranoid flights of fantasy. I was going to go hiking. Hiking with Colin would be—it would be fun, is what it would be. A good idea. Neighborly. I loved hiking. "Um, sure."

"Great!" Colin said. "I'll pick you up in half an hour?"

All my resolve ground to a halt.

"Wait—I have an errand to do in Eastsound first. Can we meet there in, I don't know, an hour?"

He paused briefly. "Sure, no problem—we can pick up some stuff for lunch too, if you don't have supplies. Where's your errand?"

"Let's meet at Island Market."

"All right. The market in an hour." He chuckled. "Bundle up. Clear means cold, in November."

Yes, I know, I've lived in the Pacific Northwest all my life, I thought. "You bet."

"You've got good shoes?"

"Don't worry about me."

I could hear the smile in his voice. "I won't. See you soon."

❧

The sheriff's substation was out by Orcas's tiny airport, on Mount Baker Road. At least, that's what Google Maps indicated; I drove by it twice before I spotted it, on the other side of Lover's Lane. It was a low blue building, looking more like a converted ranch house, complete with residential-style two-car garage, than an official headquarters of anything. *A sign would help*, I thought. Though the vehicle parked out front should have given me a clue—sort of halfway between an SUV and an ambulance, with "San Juan County Sheriff" painted on the side.

I parked next to the truck and went to the front door. It was locked.

"Huh?" I said aloud, trying the door again, as if I had been somehow mistaken. Still locked. I looked for a bell, finding none. Finally, I gave the door a tentative knock

Over at the airport, a small plane took off. I turned to watch it, then back to the door. Did I hear any noise within? I knocked again, more aggressively this time. Still nothing.

I left the front stoop and walked alongside the building, startling badly when I saw a face pressed to a small window. It was a mannequin, I realized after a moment; one of those things for practicing CPR. Was it a coincidence, or creepy island humor, to have this thing leering out at anyone nosing around the place?

Standing by the building, I rubbed my arms briefly, settling my skin back down.

What should I do? Just head on to the Island Market and go for my hike? But I didn't want to carry Megan's passport around. There wasn't time to take it back to the estate and return to town in time to meet Colin.

What kind of police station wasn't open at nine o'clock on a weekday morning?

I stared at the building again, then remembered Deputy Rankin's card. I pulled it out of my backpack, along with my cell phone, and dialed.

It was answered on the third ring. "Sheriff's Department, how may I help you?"

"Hi, I'm standing here at the office and no one's here?" I grimaced at the tentativeness in my voice, and then cleared my throat. "I need to see Deputy Rankin about something."

There was a brief pause, then, "Orcas?"

"Yes."

"One moment." I was put on hold. A full minute later, his voice came on the line. "Deputy Rankin here." That soothing, beautiful voice.

"Oh, Deputy Rankin—this is Camille Tate." At his pause, I added, "From the not-murder at Lisa Cannon's estate. I'm the next-door neighbor."

"Yes, of course. How can I help you, Ms. Tate?"

"I, um, where are you?"

He gave an almost chuckle. "On patrol. Where are you?"

"Standing in front of the police station. I mean sheriff's station. Substation. What are your open hours?"

This time the chuckle was definite. "Whenever someone is there. It's not generally open to the public. But I'm coming down Olga Road, almost to Eastsound, I can swing by. Is it an emergency?"

"No, not at all. I just need to sort of run something by you. And give you something. Things." Awkward.

"All right. Hang tight, I'll be there in five or six minutes."

"Okay." After hearing his voice, I felt oddly calmed.

After we hung up, I paced around a bit, avoiding the creepy mannequin window. Another tiny plane took off. Seemed like a lot of air traffic for such a small airport on such a small island.

A gentle breeze stirred the bushes at the edge of the parking lot. I wandered over and peered down the embankment. Beyond the bushes there was a small creek, with a little trail leading down to it. I glanced at my watch; I still had a few minutes before the deputy would get here, so I walked down to the creek. The water burbled over mossy rocks; overhead, a bird warbled in apparent response. I tossed a pebble into the creek and watched it sink to the bottom. What a pretty place this island was, even in this semi-industrial area.

I walked back up to the parking lot and looked at my watch again. Hadn't it been more than five or six minutes? If he'd meant ten, why not say so?

Finally, a familiar SUV pulled into the parking lot and drove past me. The garage door opened, then closed behind the car. A minute later, the front door opened, and Deputy Rankin stood there. "Come on in."

I followed him inside. Beyond a small entryway was an open room with three metal desks, covered in the kind of organized clutter one finds in any government office. The far wall was covered in hundreds of patches from other law enforcement agencies. I smelled coffee, and, more faintly, bleach.

Though there was nobody in the office room, he led me to a small interview room, indicating a chair for me, then taking one on the other side of the table. "So, what brings you here, Ms. Tate?"

I unzipped my pants pocket and pulled out the passport, and handed it to him, along with the scrap of note from the fireplace. "I found these in the guesthouse. Where I'm staying."

He took them, his face revealing nothing.

Sudden nerves made me chatter—if nothing else, it was a way to hold onto my voice. "You're probably wondering what kind of weirdo I am. I know that that guy wasn't murdered next door, and I even met that lady Sheila who was rehearsing with him, and she seems fine. Gruff, but fine."

He nodded like a judge, grave-faced and attentive.

Time for me to get to the point.

"I'm just really feeling like something must have happened to Megan Duquesne. The caretaker before me? My bosses don't know how to get hold of her, the neighbors don't either—her number's been disconnected. She left in such a crazy rush, you know. No warning. And without her passport! The whole thing worries me. And I didn't know what else to do about it but to bring it to you."

Deputy Rankin nodded. He studied the note carefully, and then glanced at the passport before setting them both on the table before him. "Are you certain that this note was written by Ms. Duquesne?"

"No, but it was in the fireplace of the house she was living in." *The house I am living in.* "I don't know what to think. That's why I'm here." I shrugged. "Maybe it was a prop? If she was helping the actors next door rehearse?"

He smiled gently. "Well, we thank you for this information, and for your concern. We'll look into it."

"Are you going to try to find Megan?"

"You know we cannot comment on any ongoing business of the department." Such regret in his dulcet tones.

"Right, yeah, of course." Were his eyes trying to reassure me nonetheless? In any event, I felt a sense of relief. It's always nice to hand problems off to someone else. To the proper authorities. I got to my feet. "Well, thank you. And thank you for coming in."

He stood up as well and held out his hand, giving me a courteous smile. "Not a problem, Ms. Tate—as I said, I was in the neighborhood anyway. And…I do work here." He ushered me out of the small room and to the front door. "Have a nice hike."

"What—how did you know?" I stammered.

Deputy Rankin indicated my boots, technical pants, and three layers of fleece, and pointed to my daypack. "Just a guess."

I blushed. "Yes. Thanks."

❧

Colin waited just outside the main door of the Island Market. To my dismay, his good looks hit me hard, like stepping on a rake. I'd have to get used to them all over again, it seemed. Stupid daylight.

He shook his bag. "Beef jerky, energy bars, dried fruit, and some hard-cooked eggs and other stuff. And plenty of water."

"That sounds perfect." I resisted the urge to glance at my watch again. "Am I late?"

"Nope—right on time, but I was early, so I thought I'd go ahead and shop. Besides, I'm the host: I invited you. Wasn't gonna make you buy your own lunch."

"Well, thanks."

He pointed to his truck. "Trust me enough to let me drive today?"

"Of course." I was blushing again, and cursing myself for it. This was a hike, a way to get some sun, to tire myself out so I'd sleep tonight. I needed to keep myself steady. It was his stupid looks.

I climbed in, and we set out. He turned left to head out of town, taking me down roads I hadn't seen yet.

The eastern side of the island was shadier, more heavily wooded than the West Sound area, with tall evergreens, winding roads, and little pools, inlets, and lakes everywhere. Ferns and other lush undergrowth were plentiful. The scenery was still very pretty, but I decided I preferred the openness of the west—its long meadows leading to the brilliant water.

We drove through stone gates, entering Moran State Park. "Oh, this is where that mansion is," I said, remembering what Lisa Cannon had told me.

"Rosario, yeah," Colin said. "If we get down in time and we're not too muddy, we can stop there for a drink on the way home. It's a resort now."

"A resort?"

"For the rich folk." He parked at a trailhead and turned to me with an abashed look. "Pardon me, need something in there." He nodded, indicating the glove box.

"Oh sure."

Leaning over, he reached in and fumbled around. Not quite

brushing my arm with his; not quite leaning into my lap. I held my breath, unaccountably angry with him for being that close. "There we go." He pulled out a hangtag parking permit and hung it from the rearview mirror. "Ready?"

I got out and stood by the truck, stretching my calves, catching my breath. "As ready as I can get." And I had to admit: after a sleepless night full of nightmares, worry, and my own imaginings as to Megan's fate, a hard hike sounded like a good plan.

The first few miles of the trail were deceptively easy. We climbed so gently that I almost didn't work up enough of a sweat to thaw out—it was indeed cold. "Don't worry," Colin reassured me, when we stopped to swig some water. "You'll earn your lunch."

He was right. Not long thereafter, it got crazy steep. "You know what this trail needs?" I huffed out, gasping for breath as we stopped at an overlook.

"What?"

"An escalator. Or better yet, taxi service!"

Colin laughed. "Well, you can drive to the top, but that's no fun."

"What? Now you tell me!"

"You said you liked hiking."

"I was clearly delusional. Or drunk."

We plodded on. After basically forever, we emerged at an open space. I could indeed see a parking lot through the trees. "Those cheaters," I said, but quietly, noticing a few groups of people milling about. Some were elderly; one young boy was in a wheelchair.

Colin smiled. "We'll have a better view than anyone else, don't worry."

We made our way to the pinnacle. A huge stone tower rose up, looking very impressive and military. "What is this, an army fort? Up here, in case Canada attacks or something?"

Shaking his head with a smile, Colin said, "Supposed to look like that—some old Russian thing—but it's just a CCC project."

The Civilian Conservation Corps. I'd admired their rough handiwork on so many old highways, bricked overlooks and arched tunnels, but it was hard to imagine that group of Depression-era men riding the ferries out here, living off the land, repairing the roads and creating a folly like this one. A very *tall* folly, I should add.

"Come on: the view's the best from the top floor."

"I am *not* climbing another step!" I protested, but nobody believed me, not even me. I followed him up the inner stairs, feeling like I was climbing a bell tower.

When we reached the top, the view was indeed spectacular. "Oh my goodness, this is amazing." The sun danced on the sweeping expanse of sparkling water. There were dozens of other islands, large and small, inhabited and uninhabited. Orcas was part of an archipelago.

The mainland was beyond. "What city is that?" I asked, pointing.

"Bellingham. Canada's just beyond that. We're surrounded by Canada on three sides."

"Really?"

"Well, if you want to be technical, more like two, maybe two and a half sides, depending on how you measure."

"Three sounds much more dramatic. You should just say three."

That made him laugh.

The wind blew in off the water, whipping my hair out of its ponytail and buffeting my ears as we moved slowly around the battlement, the tower's crenellations framing our views. There was one last flight of stairs, leading to a small enclosed wooden room, clearly more newly built. I followed him up. "Ah, this is better," I said, as the wind was shut out.

There were two teenage boys inside, who stopped whatever they were doing, since adults were there to ruin their fun, as adults so often do. They left, and Colin and I were alone in the tiny space.

He came to stand next to me, quite close, pointing out toward the west. "That's Vancouver Island, there."

"Really? That close?" My heart picked up speed; my arm felt the warmth from his arm. So close. And he smelled good, too. Shouldn't he smell sweaty? I knew I did. I moved away in irritation.

He took a half step back, giving me room. "No, first is the other side of Orcas; then that's San Juan beyond it; Vancouver is the one behind that. See?"

I squinted. Yes, now I could see it. The water between the different islands was hidden by the islands themselves, but the different landmasses now became clear. "Ah. Cool."

"Have you been to any of the other islands?"

"Not yet. I haven't been here that long, you know." My stomach growled.

He looked down in mock-surprise and said, "Sounds like lunchtime." Then we both heard footsteps on the stairs. Our intimate hideaway was about to be invaded anyway.

We went back to the open ground beside the tower, and joined the other view-seekers at the tower's base. A family rose up from a picnic table that was sheltered from the wind, and we moved in on it without a word or a glance. Colin opened his pack and pulled out an enticing assortment of delicacies.

"I thought you just bought hardboiled eggs and energy bars!" I said, opening a single-serving package of prosciutto and white cheese.

"And other stuff." He shrugged. "There's rabbit food too, if you'd rather."

"Let's save that for the rabbits," I said around a mouthful.

❧

All too soon, it was time to head back down the hill. "It's more fun to come up here in the summertime. Days are longer, and it's a great place to watch the sunset," he said, as we wriggled our packs back on.

"This is fine, but my muscles have seized up." I stretched my calves against the bench of the picnic table, and then bent down, waking up my hamstrings. "Ugh." I hobbled a little, trying to get the blood flowing again.

"They'll loosen up once we get walking."

Colin led the way downhill, allowing me a view of how well his slightly stretchy hiking pants conformed to his muscular physique. I found the view annoying, not exciting. Why? He wasn't putting the moves on me, there was no need to be critical of a man who had done nothing but offer friendship. Sure, I was heartbroken, but I didn't need to be a jerk about it.

We stopped at a few overlooks on the way down, but though they were lovely, they weren't nearly as impressive as the view from the top of the tower. They were much less crowded, though. We rested a bit at the last viewpoint, sitting quietly side by side, taking in the view. So many islands, large and small, rising from the shimmering water like tidy little dark-green loaves. Colin kept his distance, and I appreciated it. It let me relax. There had been too much unsaid between Kevin and me to ever let either of us relax, I realized. Evasion and disappointment and distance. But that was behind me. I was on a hike on an island, a long ferry ride away from Kevin, Seattle, and the disappointments of my more recent past.

I took a deep breath, trying to just…be.

"All right," Colin said. He stood, reaching a hand down to help me to my feet. "One final push to the car—we can make it before we lose daylight."

The steepest part of the trail was slow going, but soon we were back at the first few miles again, making that mad horses-to-the-barn dash that you do at the end of any long hike. My feet were aching, my legs were numb, I felt wrung out and ready to collapse—in other words, fantastic.

I almost missed the low "hoo-hoo" in the trees on the other side of a small ravine. "Wait," I whispered, stopping.

"What?" He stopped and followed my line of vision. "Oh."

A young owl sat on a branch, close enough for us to see his fierce gaze. He hunted from where he sat, turning his head in that impossible way owls do. He didn't seem to have spotted us; or he found us uninteresting because we weren't prey. I'd never been this close to an owl before. I liked his face, his shape, his low hoots and his cat's eyes. I wanted to pull out my phone and snap a picture of him, but the light was getting pretty low and I was afraid the motion would scare him off.

"We'd better get back," Colin whispered, after letting me watch a while.

"Okay." The owl flew off as soon as we started walking. "I think that was my favorite part."

"What, reaching flat ground?"

"No. The owl."

I was ready to collapse when we finally made the truck. "Oh, wow, am I ready for a long hot bath," I moaned.

"Don't want to stop at Rosario?"

"Hmm…" I glanced down at my muddy, sweaty, exhausted self. "You say it's a resort? How fancy is it?"

He laughed. "Well, nothing's all that fancy on the island, but, yeah, we're a little worse for the wear I guess. Rain check then?"

"Given how much it rains here, I'd say that's a safe bet."

"Deal."

We were mostly silent on the drive back up the island, but it was a comfortable, companionable silence. Once we reached Eastsound, he pulled into the Island Market parking lot beside my Honda.

I got stiffly out of the truck, stretching and groaning again. "I'm crippled for life," I complained.

"Hope not." He stood close by me—but not too close—smiling down, as I unlocked my car door. My skin was calm, and I was no longer annoyed by how handsome he was. His smile was friendly, not romantic. Safe.

"Thank you for the hike, and the lunch, and everything," I said.

"My pleasure." Still smiling.

"I owe you a meal, now. Do you want to come over for dinner or something?" I blurted, unaware that I had even had the thought before it fell out of my mouth. "I mean, like, later this week?"

"That sounds great," he said, looking serious, though his eyes were still crinkled with his smile. "Headed to America tomorrow though; back in four or five days."

"To America? Aren't we...still in America?" Had Canada finished its aggressive encroachment after all?

He laughed. "Off island, I mean, to the mainland; that's what we call it. I forget how strange that sounds." And with a mischievous grin, "To you Americans, I mean."

"Oh, okay. Well, then, after you get back? Next Friday, maybe?"

"Of course. What can I bring?"

I thought frantically. "Um—I don't know yet, I haven't figured out what I'm cooking...I haven't cooked much in that kitchen." Or anywhere, really. Takeout and ramen were more my style. What could I do with baby bok choy? Or perhaps that enormous zucchini? "I have to figure it out. I'm sort of...a not-cooking kind of a person. But I do want to return your hospitality. Lunch was awesome."

His smile turned into a laugh. "You don't need to do that. How about I cook you a nice dinner on the boat?"

"Really?"

My relief was so obvious that he laughed. "Okay, dinner at my place it is."

"All right." I shook my head, smiling. "So what can *I* bring? Don't say 'nothing.' I can at least *buy* something."

"Hmm." He paused a moment, his eyes growing vague as he lost himself in thought. I could almost see him mentally rummaging through a fridge, a pantry. Did they have those things on boats? "Why don't you go to the Island Hoppin' Brewery and pick up a growler?"

"A growler?"

"Beer."

I rolled my eyes. "I know that. I mean, what kind? Dark, light…?"

"Ask the bartender. Tell him you want something that goes with seafood but doesn't overwhelm it. You like seafood?"

"Love it."

"Good. Maybe an ale; whatever they've got that's good."

"Deal." A week would give me plenty of time to figure out where this brewery was, and choose something "good," assuming a growler wasn't seventy-five dollars or something on this crazy island.

"See you soon."

"Have a good time in America."

He laughed again. Then he swung back up into his truck and drove off.

I got into my car and just sat there a while, befuddled and pleased with myself. I was getting used to this guy. He was nice and friendly, and easy on the eyes. Well, once I got used to him each time. But I'd made my position super clear, and so had he. Just spending time with him was fun—it felt so much better than stewing in disappointment and heartache. I was ready for some friends.

You know hardly anything about him, I told myself. Yes, we had talked, but there was so much I didn't know. *This is how you get to know someone,* I answered myself. *You spend time with him. You talk, you learn about each other.*

And then…

I shook my head and started the car. The trouble was, I knew what came after *and then.* *And then* I would get frightened, or threatened, or uncomfortable, and I would vanish. *And then* he would realize I was broken, incapable of love or connection.

Better to be friends from the beginning.

And to stay that way.

CHAPTER 7

The rain did indeed return the next day, and the day after that, and the day after that. I was building a fire one afternoon, hoping to clear away some of the damp chill, when the gate bell sounded. "Yes?" I said into the intercom.

"UPS!" came a cheery voice. Oddly, it sounded just like Jen Darling. Probably just the flattening effect of the electronics.

I buzzed the driver in, then walked around to the front of the main house to greet a very familiar white panel van. Redheaded Jen Darling hopped out, wearing a black slicker and grinning at me.

"UPS?" I asked. "I thought you were FedEx."

"That too. I've been DHL a couple of times, but we don't get a lot of international here."

I looked her over. No package, no clipboard. Of course no uniform. "You deliver for everyone?"

She nodded. "Sometimes the post office too. Stuff comes in, somebody has to bring it around."

"Okay. Um, so you have a package for me?"

She laughed and shook her head. "Oh, no, I was out making a delivery at Deer Harbor, and I thought I'd stop by and say hi. Are you busy?"

I couldn't help grinning. Stop by, without calling? They really did that here! It was like living in a sitcom. "No, just trying to avoid my screenplay. Come on in."

We went around to the guesthouse. "Have a seat," I told her, then waved to the fireplace. "I'm trying to conjure up the sun here."

"Great!"

Within a minute or two, the paper and kindling had caught. I laid a few larger logs over them. "Do you want anything to drink? I guess you can't have a beer, on the job…"

She looked sad, but nodded. "Yeah, probably not. Tea would be nice, if you've got it."

"Tea it is." That would be warmer anyway.

She followed me into the kitchen. "That's one heckuva zucchini."

It lay there on the counter, looking humongous and very green. "Yes. It just appeared on my doorstep one day."

"Like an abandoned baby?"

"Exactly. I have no idea what to do with it. I don't actually cook."

"Do you think it's a…message?" She tilted her head and grinned; I laughed. Then she frowned. "It can't be from someone's garden—not in November."

"Huh. You're right. That is weird."

"Well, never look a gift zucchini in the mouth, that's what I say."

I put on the kettle and brought my few boxes out of the cabinet. "Earl Grey, Magnificent Mint, or Orange Spice."

"Ooh, Orange Spice." She took a seat at the small kitchen table, looking around. "This place is really nice. I've never been back here. I thought I'd been everywhere on the island, but the Brixtons just built this guesthouse a few years ago, when they remodeled the big one."

"I like it too," I said, coming to sit across from her. "At first I was disappointed when I learned I had to move out of the big house, but I did spend a couple of nights there, and it was too big. It's kind of creepy and lonely for one person. The scale's all wrong."

She looked at me, her eyes kind, warm. "You're not used to living alone?"

I shrugged. "Well, yes and no. Before my last boyfriend, I lived alone—but in crowded apartment buildings in crowded cities. Alone here is…more alone. You know?"

"I sure do. That's why it's important to make friends." She gave me a brilliant smile. "And to keep busy with a few jobs. Gets you out in the world."

"My jobs both keep me here. Alone." I let that settle in. Could I do something about it?

The kettle whistled; I got up and poured two mugs of Orange Spice, and brought them to the table with spoons and a dish for the teabags.

"You should come into town to write," she said. "Bring your laptop. Caretaking doesn't mean spending all your time here, does it?"

"No, I'm sure it doesn't—I just have to be around enough to keep an eye on things." I stirred the teabag around in the hot water, watching the little eddies of color. "I don't think I write very well in public, though. I thought I'd enjoy the privacy more." I looked up at her. "I don't hate it, but…well, I haven't been here that long. Probably I'll get used to it."

"Yeah, probably you will."

"I guess my big problem is I haven't really done much writing yet. I keep deleting what I type and starting over."

"I could never be a writer," she said. "I could never sit still that long."

I laughed. "I don't sit still very well either."

We both perked up our ears as the sounds of…something… filtered into the house. Voices? It was faint, but definitely there.

"Do your neighbors fight a lot?" she asked, after a minute.

I frowned, straining to hear. "They're probably just rehearsing again. That's Lisa Cannon's estate next door."

"Right. All her thespians." But she seemed a little wary. She shook her head and smiled. "How about a magic trick?"

People made strange requests on this island. "I don't know any magic tricks."

She smiled. "I do. I can make your giant zucchini disappear, and reappear as…zucchini muffins."

"That," I said, "sounds like my favorite magic trick of all time." I smiled at her. "This really *is* a different place, isn't it?"

Jen looked at me with a serious expression. "It is, it really is. And not only do you either love it or hate it—I'm convinced that the island knows *you*. I mean, not you specifically, but anyone. People come here and they either feel at home at once, or…not welcome."

My heart rate picked up a little at her words. I must have frowned, because she went on: "What is it, Cam?"

I looked up at her. "I know what you mean, I think, but I'm also a little confused."

"How so?"

"I love it here—I felt comfortable right away, and it's so gorgeous, and peaceful. But…there are weird things happening, too."

"Weird? Like what? The zucchini?"

Where to begin? "Well, yeah, that. And coffee. And Lisa, next door."

Jen rolled her eyes. "No-jobber extraordinaire. She gets packages nearly every day." She leaned forward. "What's she done that's weird?"

"Not her, exactly. She's actually been nice to me, very welcoming."

"Oh, don't get me wrong—she's nice—it's just…she lives here but she's not *of* here. Know what I mean?"

Would any no-jobber be *of* here, in Jen's eyes? "She founded the local theater, right?"

Jen nodded. "Yeah, one of them. I know she's trying. And everyone likes her, she's doing a lot for the community. But...it's all Seattle money, Seattle plays, Seattle actors..." She shrugged. "For a *repertory* theater, she sure imports a lot of talent."

"She does surround herself with...interesting people," I ventured.

She caught my tone. "Ah. Who?"

"This woman Sheila, for one. Do you know her?"

Jen shook her head. "Not really. She signs for the packages, more often than not. What's her deal?"

I sighed. "I don't know, exactly. Lisa's invited me over a few times, but every time I go there, it seems like Sheila is just...hovering around. Unhappily. She kind of freaks me out."

"Freaks you out?"

Okay, stop dancing around, just tell her. "My first morning here, I thought I saw Sheila shoot someone."

"Shoot?" Her eyebrows rose. "Like, with a camera?"

"No. Like with a gun. Murdering him. Turns out they were just rehearsing for some upcoming play, she was helping him run lines, but...it still feels weird, and unsettling. And I can't figure out what play it might be. It's not their next one, I know that. And...there's more things."

She nodded, clearly not very impressed with what I'd said so far, but being polite.

So I told her about the missing Megan, and her not-missing passport; about the crumpled-up letter in the fireplace to Gregory; about taking all that to the sheriff's deputy, and his unruffled response. It felt surprisingly good to unburden myself. The only thing I didn't tell her about was my inconvenient superpower. Chameleoning was hard to explain, and even harder to understand. If I didn't absolutely have to go there, it was always better not to.

As recent events with Kevin had demonstrated, all too clearly.

As I talked, Jen's eyes widened so far I thought they'd pop right out of her head. "Oh, gracious goodness," she said when I finished. "A 'murder'? The note? The passport? And you're just sitting on that, not telling a soul? Poor Cam!"

"Well, except Deputy Rankin," I said.

"What did he say?"

"Nothing. It's an..."

"...active investigation. But seriously, Cam. Do you think they're really hiding something over there in the house that tech millions built?" She waved in the direction of the Cannon estate.

"Good grief, I hope not." I thought about it further. "What would they be hiding?"

"Oh, gosh, all sorts of things! Boats in and out all the time, all those people coming and going, staying there half the time instead of someplace in town, packages arriving every day..." Her grin was growing ever wider. It was starting to worry me. She smacked the table with the palm of her hand; her curls shook with the reverberation. "I think we should *investigate*."

"Are you *kidding* me?" I shook my head hard enough to hurt my neck. "The deputy pretty much told me to mind my own business."

"Where's the fun in that?" Jen was already on her feet, draining the last of her tea and setting the cup on the table. Not listening to a word I said. "Come on," she said, reaching down to drag me up to standing as well. "Let's go for a walk."

"No way, no way, no way," I protested, as she was yanking me toward the door.

"We'll just walk down to the water," she said. "It's a shared dock, isn't it?" She grabbed my jacket and thrust it at me. "Lovely day for a walk."

"It's raining."

"No it's not." She opened the door; indeed, the traitorous rain had let up. I even saw patches of blue among the clouds. "Is that Gregory fellow's boat still there?"

"It's not *at* the shared dock, I told you—it went into some trees. I didn't see where it tied up. I have no idea if it's still there."

She grinned. "Even better! We'll stay on the Brixton property, like we have every right to. Maybe we can see Lisa's private dock from the shared one."

I groaned even as I surrendered, putting my arms through my jacket sleeves. "I can't believe I'm doing this. You'll get us both killed."

"Me?" she said, mock-innocent. "Nobody's dead. At least…as far as we know."

She was absolutely loving this.

❧

We tromped across the dormant, soggy lawn and down to the waterfront, then walked out onto the shared pier. It was just as it had been on my first day here: the tied-up, covered rowboat; no other boats. "See?" I said, gesturing with my arms at the open space. "Nothing to look at here."

"Nice day, though," Jen observed, looking out over the view. A beam of sun had broken through the quickly scattering clouds, sparkling as it touched the water. The breeze was almost pleasant.

I gave Jen a suspicious glance. She looked far too innocent. I followed her gaze. "Yeah. Orcas Island is truly lovely."

"Oh, it's one of the garden spots of the world. A hidden gem. We live in a wonderland of beauty." She stretched out her arms in an expansive gesture that took it all in; the weathered dock, the sloping lawn, the tall stands of evergreens, the sparkling water of the bay, and…the waterfront that belonged to the property next door.

"Okay then!" I said, brightly. "You've seen the shared dock. Want another cup of tea before you go back to your obviously very busy schedule today?" I walked back up the pier to the beach and started heading up the hill, stopping when it was clear she wasn't following me. "Come on."

She peered intently through the trees. "I think maybe I see something…maybe a boat…"

I shrugged. "Of course. There has to be a place for a boat to tie up there. I told you that."

"I just want to be sure." She practically skipped off the dock and started walking along the rocky beach toward Lisa Cannon's place.

The property line was clear enough, even without any fence. "I'm not responsible for what happens to you if you get caught trespassing," I called out.

Jen Darling stopped and looked up at me, adorable mischief on her face. "Oh, come on, Cam. Lisa likes me. She likes you too—she's given you an open invitation to come by any time, right? We're just going for a walk along the shoreline. Nobody's *trespassing*."

Grumbling to myself, I made my way back down the slope and joined her.

We pushed our way through a thicket of wild shrubbery and emerged onto a suspiciously well-groomed bit of lawn. We couldn't quite see Lisa's house from here, but another few feet and I was sure we would. "How does she get the grass to stay so green this time of year?" I muttered.

"Witchcraft and sorcery. Or maybe she's programmed it to grow like this," Jen said. "Look, there's her private dock. And there's a powerboat moored at it!"

"Of course Lisa would have a boat of her own," I pointed out. "There, you've seen it, can we go?"

"Yep." But she pressed on, just kept walking toward it. "Is this the boat you saw come in that day?"

Well, I had to admit, I was a bit curious myself. I kept walking, keeping up with Jen as I looked at the boat. "Maybe? I'm not much of an expert on boats." I studied it as we drew closer, in between nervous glances up the hill. Still couldn't see Lisa's house from here, it was blocked by trees. Come to think of it, I hadn't

noticed any dock from her house, the times I'd been in there—
not that I'd been looking for one. Maybe we were safe here. Were
we? "It was about this size, I guess. I don't remember the color."
This boat was that sort of white-fiberglassy color so common in
smaller craft. It had an outboard motor, and space for maybe
three people in it. Four if they were cozy. A little windshield. Not
much else.

Jen frowned slightly and spoke softly. "This is not a rich person's boat."

She had a point. I wished I'd paid more attention to the boat
that morning, but the whole thing had been so unexpected, so
startling. It had been barely sunrise, and he'd been coming from
the southeast—the light had been behind him. He'd worn a hat.
He'd been shot, except not.

I wouldn't have been able to pick him out of a crowd, either.

Jen finally glanced up toward where the house was. It wasn't
visible to us, so she must have decided that we weren't visible to
it. She headed down to the tiny dock, walked out on it, and bent
down to peer into the boat.

I followed her, stopping halfway out, keeping an eye out behind us.

"Funny, no name," she said.

"What?"

"Most craft have names."

I looked. The boat had a string of numbers on its hull—registration, I imagined—and a brand name, nearly worn away by
weather and water and time, but no boat-specific name. "Do
they have to?"

"No, but they almost always do. It's kind of weird for it not to
have one." She turned and grinned at me again. "Almost like it's
incognito."

"Or like it's such a punky little boat, nobody bothered naming
it."

"Or that." She shrugged, then lifted a foot to step over into the boat.

"What are you doing?!" I hissed. "Get *out* of there!"

She paused, looking back at me. "What? I'm just going to look." She finished stepping on board; the boat swayed gently as it accepted her weight. "Come on, there's room for you too."

"Not on your life." I took a few steps back, returning to stand on the grass, crossing my arms over my chest. We shouldn't have even gone out on that little dock. Yes, I knew we were already trespassing, even here; but somehow, out there seemed ever so much worse.

"Suit yourself." She sat down on one of the benches and started rummaging around under the windshield, near the controls.

"What are you looking for?" I edged a little closer, trying to see.

"Something. Anything."

I glanced nervously behind us again. The woods were quiet; the slope up to Lisa's house was steep and forbidding. Wooden stairs were built down along the side closest to the Brixton estate—no walking down any muddy hillside for Ms. Cannon and company. All was quiet up there, but my skin was crawling.

"Ooh," Jen said, her voice muffled from having her head stuck almost entirely under the dashboard or whatever you call that part on a boat.

"What?" I couldn't help myself, I stepped back out onto the dock again. My skin started to tingle. I rubbed my arms, self-soothing. *Calm, okay, quiet, good, safe,* I crooned in my head. The tingles settled, mostly.

"Paperwork. Here." She fumbled a bit more, then emerged, clutching a handful of wrinkled papers.

"I'm sure that's the registration and proof of insurance or whatever," I said.

She looked back at me with amusement. "You really do know nothing about boats, huh?"

I shrugged, embarrassed. "Well, no. I've never lived near the water."

"I thought you moved here from Seattle?"

"Yeah, from an apartment in Queen Anne. The water is kind of a remote decoration, or a thing that interrupts the flow of traffic. Only super rich people actually *live* on the water."

"Ah." Clutching the papers, she stepped off the boat and came to stand next to me on the dock. "That sounds so weird to me. Water belonging to the rich." She shuffled through the papers. "Just the title and registration."

"Isn't that what I said?"

Jen grinned. "Aha! Didn't you say the dude's name was Gregory? The one in Megan's note, the dude who got shot but didn't get shot? Gregory, right?"

"Yeah." I leaned forward to see the papers, now more intrigued than anything else. This craft was registered to a Gregory Baines. There was also a business name: Tempera Holdings, LLC. The address was a post office box in Seattle.

"Ooh, it's a mystery!" Jen was still grinning happily. "We need to find out more about this Gregory Baines. Come on—let's go back to your place and Google him."

"Fine." Anything to get off Lisa Cannon's property. Nice as she was, I had no idea how we would explain this if she caught us here.

She, or Sheila. My skin started up again. We needed to get to a safe place, and soon, or I'd be in trouble. Jen started to walk up the dock. "Wait a second," I said. "Put those papers back."

"No one will miss them. They were tucked way up inside, in a little compartment."

"Why do we need them? We've got his name!"

She folded them and shoved them into a pocket. "What about the business name, and the address? We'll need all this for our research." She started walking along the shoreline back to the Brixtons'. "You can put them back later."

I shivered. Trespass again, just to put something back? What was this girl getting me into? My hands were going, but she didn't notice because I tucked them into my armpits and got moving. The further we got from the scene of the crime/not crime, the better I felt.

We were actually laughing as we walked, enjoying the sun on the water and each other's company.

ↄ

Back at the house, an internet search revealed nobody special by the name of Gregory Baines—or, rather, far too many people. According to an image search, more than half of them were black; this guy, from my impressions, was white. But even narrowing it by race didn't help. "Too common a name," I said.

Jen moved on to Tempera Holdings, LLC. Nothing whatsoever came up. "Okay, that *is* weird," she said. "Even if they're not a public company, they should have a business license, and that would come up."

"Have you ever tried searching on a P.O. box?" I sat back. "That's that, then?"

Jen frowned, gazing back at me. "Just a momentary setback." Then she pulled out her cell phone and checked the time. "Whoah, I gotta get back on the road." She leapt to her feet, snatched up the zucchini, and pulled me into a quick hug. "Thanks for the tea! This has been *so much* fun!"

Fun?

In another moment, she was gone, white panel van motoring back down the driveway.

I pushed the button to let her out—which, now that I thought about it, struck me as a strange feature. Didn't automatic gates usually open, well, automatically if you approached them from the inside?

Unless you want to control all comings and goings, I thought. If you really wanted to protect your privacy, you needed to be in charge of guests leaving as well as arriving. If people could just drive off whenever, what would stop them from letting anyone else in?

How had Deputy Rankin gotten out, that first morning, come to think of it? Did cops have special gate-opening overrides in their cars?

I shook my head. Too strange, all of this.

But Jen was right. It had been kind of fun.

Jen's visit was a brilliant distraction, but then of course she left, and then time did that thing where it slowed waaaaaayyy down. I had to rebuild the fire, but after I got it going again, the hours just crept by. The screenplay would not write itself, I was hungry even though I'd already eaten more than enough—the day would just *not* end. My brother Cliff, off on the other side of the world, was hardly keeping up his end of the Words with Friends bargain, going hours between moves even when I knew it was daytime in Thailand. He did send an email saying he'd love to Skype some time, but he was too busy right now; he'd let me know when he could.

Which meant only one thing. I'd exhausted all my distractions, and it was time to write.

CHAPTER 8

The next morning, the San Juan County Sheriff's Department continued to not phone me to report on the progress of their no-doubt intense and ongoing investigation into the mysterious disappearance of Megan Duquesne. Jen Darling didn't drop by with important information gleaned from the registration she'd carried away. No one left anything on my doorstep.

In fact, nothing at all happened, except that I wrote some more of my screenplay.

Well, I erased the whole first scene and rewrote it, then erased half of that. Now that I knew a real producer was interested in seeing it, I could hardly function. I felt like Lisa Cannon was standing over my shoulder as I wrote, tsk-ing and shaking her head. It sucked. I sucked. I could never be a writer. Whatever had possessed me to imagine I could be a writer?!

But I had a title, thanks to Lisa. *Salon Confessional.*

Midday, I went into town. I needed groceries, and there was also the issue of finding an affordable bottle of amazing wine to take to Lisa Cannon. Ha ha. I hadn't made it to her happy hour yet—I'd been too discombobulated by my sudden chameleoning on the path, found myself abruptly on a hike with Colin the next day, and then it rained like the dickens for a few days after that—but I had to go soon, so she didn't think I was rude, or un-grateful. And I was going to bring a bottle of wine, dang it, never mind what she'd said or how ambrosial her wines were. I wasn't a complete freeloader.

There was a small wine shop on North Beach Road, just to the far side of an adorable little park. In my experience, specialty wine shops were the most expensive places on the planet; but maybe the Island Market's prices wouldn't look so bad if I started here. Anyway, I was still on my mission to explore my new com-munity.

A bell over the door gave a cheerful jangle as I opened it, and again as I closed the door tight behind me. I wiped my boots on the doormat and looked around.

Racks of bottles lined the walls, with more bottles stacked on haphazard shelves below them, and unopened cases shoved everywhere, with bottles stacked on them too. The whole place smelled pleasant and musty, like a cellar, though there was a large window at the front.

Behind the counter, an old man sat on a stool, looking at a magazine. "Can I help you?" he asked, smiling at me.

"Oh, I'm just browsing for now, thank you." When you accept-ed help, when you engaged, it was so much harder to get out of buying something.

"All right, you let me know." With a merry twinkle in his eyes, he returned to his reading.

I stared at all the bottles, pretending I knew anything at all about fine wines. Most of the wines on the wall racks had little note cards under them, with carefully handwritten descriptions, though in much plainer language than I was accustomed to in wine-speak. And more interesting. "Strong and fruity; good with cheddar cheese and Triscuits." "Light, a little thin; you'll want to drink this one in summer, and make sure it's very cold." "Put it away and see if it gets any better with time." I snorted at that one.

Even more surprising, though, were the prices. Most of them, anyway; the upper shelves held bottles marked forty or sixty dollars or even more, but the lower shelves were full of wines I could actually afford.

Would Kevin have loved this place, or would he have found it a disappointment?

Well, I loved it.

The old man looked up as I passed closer to the counter. A ratty little dog slept at his feet. I smiled at him—the man, not the dog—and said, "Actually, I could use a recommendation. I need a wine to take to a, um, friend's house. And not too..."

"Not too expensive?" he finished for me, with an understanding smile.

"Exactly."

"Red or white?"

I thought about it. She'd served me red, but had also mentioned setting out a variety. "White, maybe; something to have before dinner. With appetizers."

"Ah, of course. I bet I have just the thing." He came out from behind the counter and went to an aisle toward the back of the store, muttering under his breath as he picked up, then rejected, three or four bottles. "It's back here somewhere..." He pulled another one out, wiped the dust off, and peered at it more closely. "Here you go," he said, handing it over to me. "A nice Chenin Blanc from South Africa."

It had a pretty label. I glanced discreetly at the price tag. "Nine dollars?" I blurted. "That's—that's great."

"Good!" He started to shuffle back to the front of the store, then asked, "Is that all you need? I got some interesting Syrah in the other day. There won't be any dinner?"

"No, just this for now, thanks. I'll be back, though. I'm caretaking out in West Sound, so you'll see me again."

"Caretaking, that's marvelous! Who for?"

"The Brixtons, Emmett and Diana—do you know them?"

He frowned, thinking. "Can't say as I do."

"I don't know how often they get out here."

"Ah, summer people." He grinned, shrugged, and started punching numbers into an ancient cash register. "I'm not always fancy enough for the summer folk."

"Your prices are very competitive," I said.

"Gotta keep folks comin' in. The stories only do so much."

"Stories?"

He looked up at me and grinned. "Just heard a new one the other day. You want to hear it?"

"Um, sure."

"Okay, so, there was this young couple, Bob and, er, Elaine. They got married—big church wedding, fancy cake, the whole works. It was a very nice wedding. Very nice. Whole island talked about it."

I nodded, smiling at this odd man.

"And so then, like you do after a wedding, they went away on their honeymoon." Now his eyes had that glint again. *Oh no, what have I gotten myself into?* I thought.

"When they got back," he went on, "Elaine phoned her mother, Lucy. Lives just up the road here, down towards Moran. Lucy asked, 'How was the honeymoon, dearest?'

"'Oh, Ma,' Elaine replied, 'the honeymoon was wonderful. So romantic…'

"'Oh, honey, that's nice,' Lucy said.

"But then Elaine burst out crying. 'Ma, as soon as we got home, Bob started using the most ghastly language…saying things I've never heard before! I mean, all these awful four-letter words! You've got to come get me and take me home! Please, Ma.'

"'Calm down, Elaine!' said her mother. 'Tell me, what could be so awful? What four-letter words?'

"But Elaine could hardly speak, she was sobbing so hard. Finally, she managed to pull it together long enough to whisper, 'Oh, Ma…words like dust, wash, cook, and iron.'" The old man guffawed loud enough to startle the little dog awake.

I groaned and rolled my eyes. "Oh, wow, um. Thanks." Not only was that wretched, I was fairly sure I'd heard it before. I shook my head and put my hand out. "My name's Cam, by the way."

He shook my hand. "I'm Porter. I know! Perfect, right? What else could I do but open a wine shop?"

I laughed. "Right. Well, it's nice to meet you, Porter. I'll see you again soon, I'm sure."

"Good luck with your little gathering! Come back and tell me how the wine was."

"I will!"

The door chimes rang me back out onto the street.

❦

I spent the afternoon working on the screenplay, trying to ignore the noise of next door's rehearsals—they must have been working on a very dramatic part of the play today. I knew my first scene was a jumbled mess, but I decided I could fix it later. I needed to move more into the heart of the story. Maybe once I had a better sense of where it was going, the early parts would fall into place more easily.

So Felicia went downtown to meet the nephew's ex-girlfriend at the night club. Only…she wasn't there. So she sat at the bar a while. The bartender was cute, and seemed super extra interested in her. Was this suspicious? Or was it just the low-cut blouse Felicia had worn, trying to blend in here? She drank a Cosmopolitan, nursing it slowly, refusing a second one. She wanted to keep her wits about her. Something, *something*, was not right here. She had a feeling. Just a sense. She discreetly glanced into her tiny evening bag, but there were no messages on her cell phone. The bartender kept smiling at her…

I rolled my eyes, highlighted the entire scene, and hit 'delete'. "Jeez, you hack," I said to myself. Not only was the scene derivative, it was totally boring. Nothing happened at all. I didn't know what was supposed to happen. It was like I was chattering nervously, but in the form of writing.

Oh, look at the time!

I took the Chenin Blanc out of my fridge, checked in the mirror to make sure I didn't have baby bok choy in my teeth, and walked down the path to Lisa's house. Today's light rain had tapered off in the late afternoon, but it was dark out here; I used the flashlight app on my phone to light the way. Awkward, but functional. Probably I should look around the house for an actual flashlight. They'd be forty-five dollars at the store, I was sure.

When I emerged from the little bit of woods, I could see that her house was lit up, but I didn't hear anything. So, they rehearsed at the top of their lungs all day and then whispered during happy hour?

I rang the doorbell, hearing the gentle chimes echo within. Then I waited. For what seemed like kind of too long. If it was a standing invitation, should I just let myself in? At least try the doorknob?

Before I could decide what to do, Lisa opened the door. She was wearing canvas pants that were stained and ragged at the hemlines, and a rumpled T-shirt, yet she still managed to look elegantly put-together. "Cam! How wonderful, come in!" She stepped back, drawing the door wide open.

I walked in, holding out the bottle of wine like a talisman. "I, uh…" I looked around. No one else was here. "…thought you had a gathering…?"

Lisa Cannon laughed, making me feel relaxed and comfortable just by the magic of her evident delight. "I do! But sometimes no one shows up. The whole gang was here all day, workshopping a project, then they hied off into town for dinner right at five. So I was going to paint a little. But I'd much rather have a glass of wine with you." She reached out to take the bottle. "What do you have here?"

"Oh, well, I don't really know wines, but—"

She stopped in her tracks, then wheeled around to face me. Her grey eyes bored into mine. "Camille Tate. You listen to me."

"I...what?"

"You are an intelligent, creative, interesting human being. You have taste and opinions and style, and those things matter. You knew what you liked when I served you my friend's Rattlesnake Hills wine and the sipping chocolate. Even if you'd never heard of them before. Those tastes are valid, and you should *never* apologize for them." She softened a little, holding up the wine. "Now, if you like this wine, that's all I need to know. All right?"

"Um...I haven't tasted it yet. The fellow at the wine store... um..."

Her laughter rang out, echoing off the high ceiling. "Oh, Cam! There I went, off on my high horse again. You'll have to forgive me." She gave me a sheepish look. "I'm just so tired of smart, qualified women *apologizing* for everything, every single day—apologizing for *existing*, even. I saw it in the industry far, far too much. But it's everywhere. And it's wrong." She gave a little shrug. "And we're standing here talking when we should be drinking this undoubtedly delicious wine." She turned and went to the long counter separating the open kitchen from the sitting area below, and picked up a corkscrew. "Sit!"

I sat.

She joined me a moment later, handing me a big glass of the pale golden liquid. "Thank you," I said.

"No, thank *you*, for bringing it." She raised her glass to mine, and we clinked. "Last time we toasted to new neighbors—this time we should drink to your patience and generosity."

"I can't toast myself!" I protested, but sipped anyway. Yum.

"So, the wine shop," she said after a moment. "Porter?"

"Yeah."

Lisa noted my smile. "He tell you any stories?"

"Indeed he did. You want to hear it?"

"I most certainly do not."

When we had finished laughing, she added, "Yes, this island does have its fair share of characters. Have you met Paige Berry yet?"

"No."

She shook her head and rolled her eyes. "You will."

"Who is she?"

Lisa studied me, an amused glint in her eye. "I think I'll let you discover her without any introduction. It's better that way."

"O-kay." I grinned back at her and sipped my wine. "Fine, be that way."

She leaned forward and nudged a platter of crackers and cheese toward me—I hadn't even noticed it on the huge coffee table, amid the elegant glass ornaments and healthy orchids laden with blooms in vibrant purples and pinks. "Here, eat; those freeloaders in town won't want it when they get back."

I partook, and thought a moment. Hadn't Jen said something about the actors not staying in town? "So, are they all staying here?" Other than rough-around-the-edges Sheila, I'd never seen anyone else here. Well, except for Gregory, the guy who had played dead.

Lisa shrugged. "The troupe pretty much camps here when we're in rehearsals, and for the first few weeks of a show. Especially the ones who come from off-island. I have an embarrassment of guest bedrooms and the island is expensive, so it makes sense."

"That's nice of you." I ate another cracker. "You must love this so much more than working with sexist jerks in tech."

"Ha!" She raised her glass in agreement. "You better believe it. Yes, my life is so much better now."

I glanced around. The room was just as impressive as the other times I'd been here, and yet, something about it seemed…lonely? I thought about my talk during tea yesterday with Jen Darling. Before we'd devolved into trespassing. "You don't have a partner or anything?"

"I was married right out of college. It lasted ten years." She said it like she was talking about the weather. "Haven't gone there since; not a lot of opportunity in tech, despite the gender ratio. Speaking of sexist jerks. What about you?"

"Never married. Just left a relationship, very recently—or, well, he left me, sort of. It's why I moved here. Or at least why I was open to it."

"Oh, Cam, I am so sorry."

Now I was sorry I'd brought the whole business up. I was so terrible at small talk. "So Lisa, I was wondering—even though they hired me, I don't really know the Brixtons all that well. I know that the last caretaker was only here a few weeks. But did you know the one before that?"

She studied me a moment. "They didn't have one before that."

"They didn't? But who—?"

"The son lived there." A slight smile. "JoJo, as he is familiarly known."

"JoJo? Seriously?" The vampire in the crimson room? Well, that explained the recent pot-smoke smell.

She gave a gentle laugh. "Perhaps he will grow out of it some day. But for now..." She shook her head and took a cracker, putting a slice of white cheese on it and nibbling thoughtfully.

"Is he...nice? I don't know the kids at all. There's two, right?"

Lisa nodded, chewing. "Yes, JoJo and Clary—Clarice."

Clary, right. Not Carrie. "I suppose I'll meet them at Thanksgiving. They're all coming out."

"They are? Oh, good. It'll be nice to see them. Are you going to be joining them?"

I shook my head. "No, I don't think so; my own parents are thinking about maybe coming out. If they do, we'll be crowded over there." Should I invite her too? Would the Brixtons? Or would she have a big meal with all her actors? I liked Lisa, but I hardly knew her.

"How nice for you! Have they been to the islands before?" She got up and fetched the wine bottle, topping us off.

"No, none of us have, I mean had. Before me." I waved a hand near my glass as she poured. "Not much more for me—I should get home and make dinner soon." Before she could interpret that as a hint, I added, "I've got a big writing evening planned."

"Excellent! Don't forget you're going to show me some scenes."

"Oh, I am not in the least forgetting that."

She sipped, seeming lost in thought again a moment, then said, "To answer your question: yes, JoJo is a perfectly nice fellow, though complicated, I'd have to say. Actually, both children are, in different ways. I see that often, in people born to privilege. Do you know what I mean?"

"I do, I do indeed," I said. I thought about the extremely detailed house manual. About Diana Brixton's precise instructions about her hair, delivered anew at each appointment, no matter that I had gotten it right dozens of times already. As evidenced by her generous tips, and continued patronage. "Perhaps the Brixtons were…complicated parents, as well."

Lisa smiled at me. "Of that I have no doubt. Much as I admire Diana, I would not want to be her daughter."

"Yeah."

"It's brave of you to work for her," she said.

"Well, I like her too. But it's not like I have to see her every day." I gave a polite smile, not wanting to trash talk my new employer.

"Well, if you ever get tired of her, there's always me." Lisa smiled, and there was a hint of something in that smile, something steely and acquisitive. "I'm always open to the idea of a new personal assistant. Sheila is dutiful and flexible, but as you've seen, she can be a little…abrupt at times."

I almost spit out my cracker. "Sheila is your personal assistant?" Scenes from a few movies flashed through my brain, mixed with memories of the personal assistants who called the salon to book appointments for their bosses in Seattle. Weren't PAs supposed to be obsequious, fawning, and lovably codependent? Sheila seemed gruff and surly and not at all what I'd expect for a woman like Lisa. I'd thought she was a, I don't know, handy person or something?

"Yes. She's a diamond in the rough. With an accent on the rough, I guess you'd say." She winked at me, Lisa actually winked. "We're working on the polishing."

I had no idea what to say, so I just sipped my wine, trying to put together the pieces. And then my glass was empty. "I should let you get back to your painting, Lisa. I have my own creative endeavors to ignore. I mean work on."

She laughed, and rose to her feet in that swift and graceful way she had, to show me to the door. "You may interrupt me any time, Camille. You're a pleasure."

I was actually blushing from the compliment on the path back to the guesthouse, warmed by the wine and by her generosity of spirit. I raised my head and walked with confidence past the site of the not-murder. My skin wasn't crawling—maybe because I'd finally accepted that what I'd seen really was a rehearsal, or maybe because I'd had too much wine.

But setting aside the wine, I had started to understand that there was no danger here. This was a friendly place, and an eccentric place, but for all intents and purposes, I was safe here. And as odd as some of the local habits were, I had some optimistic idea that I might fit in.

I reached the circle of light by the main house's back door, where another giant zucchini sat on the doormat, propped against the door.

"What is it with this *produce*?"

"Hey." Sheila's voice, gruff and a little scornful. I must have jumped a mile. "I gotta talk to you a second." She had on a bulging plaid shirt jacket, and kept throwing nervous glances over her shoulder. "Crazy stuff happens. Girl living alone way out here... if you scream, no one hears you." She reached for her zipper. What was in that lumpy jacket? The wine had been surprisingly strong and I couldn't vanish, even if I wanted to.

I pressed myself against the door. The only weapon at hand was the zucchini. "Um…what?"

Sheila reached inside her jacket. "I think you need protection."

"I…"

She pulled out a leggy, squirming young cat with orange fur, a white face and green eyes.

Not a gun. Not a knife. A kitten. "With *that*?"

"Yeah." Sheila held it out by the scruff of its neck. "Cats are smarter than you think. It was whatsername's."

"Whatsername?"

"You know. The one who was over here before you?"

"Do you mean Megan?"

"Yeah. Megan. She left it when she took off, and it showed up over at Lisa's, and the boss lady isn't so much for animals. I been hiding it, more or less. But I can't keep it."

She left her *kitten*? Her passport and her *kitten*?

The kitten mewled. It was clearly tired of dangling by the scruff of its neck, and probably too old to be safely held that way. I scooped it into my arms, and felt sharp little claws dig into my arm as if to say it would not be letting go anytime soon. "Does it have a name?"

"Him. His name is James. I took him to the vet and got him fixed. That kept him quiet for a while, but he's all healed up now, and I can't keep him cooped up inside."

Well, that was an odd name for a cat, but whatever. "I hate to disappoint you, but if Lisa Cannon doesn't like cats in her house, can you imagine what Diana Brixton would do?"

Sheila shook her head, not meeting my eyes. Her face showed enormous irritation. "Listen, here's the deal. He's an outside cat. All you have to do is feed him and take him to the vet if he looks sick. He doesn't even have to come inside. He just needs someone to feed him. The way I see it, you look out for him, he looks out for you."

"I...I don't know, Sheila." He was settled into my arms, purring so ferociously that I felt the vibration throughout my abdomen. "What a motor you have. What should I do with you, handsome James?" He looked up when I spoke his name, and I rubbed him under his little white chin. His white paws worked on my arm, kneading for all he was worth, and his green eyes closed in languid feline contentment.

When I looked up, Sheila was gone.

The kitten was not.

CHAPTER 9

Two days later, I finally decided to make the trek into town to attempt writing in public.

I'd been putting it off, not wanting to figure out yet another new thing. But I wasn't making enough progress working alone. And even though James was doing his best to entertain/distract me by springing around the house on the long legs of an older kitten, pouncing on my foot, his tail, a shadow, the power cord with gymnastic agility, I was getting lonely for human companionship.

Colin had texted: he'd spent a few extra days in "America," but he was back now, could we have dinner Friday? *Yes*, I wrote back. Which was great, but didn't help my loneliness today.

Jen hadn't stopped by again, and things seemed quieter than usual next door. I supposed I could have gone over for another "happy hour," but I didn't want to impose on Lisa's generous spirit, no matter how much she seemed to like me.

I had to go find people before I became completely weird. Maybe I'd look for a community bulletin board where I could post a "free to a good home" note for James, or find a flyer from a place that did cat rescue. Or something. Because I couldn't just keep this little cat. No matter how fetchingly he gamboled and tumbled, chasing his tail in the sunlight.

Despite what Sheila had told me, I wasn't excited about leaving James outside, where he could kill songbirds or wander up onto the road, but I did it. I knew I couldn't leave a cat in the guesthouse when I wasn't home, so it was time to let him off on his own.

"I make you no promises, James. I don't know when I'll be home, and I assume you don't either. But I hope you know you're welcome." I opened the door and he gave me barely a glance before scampering off to follow a flying insect.

I hadn't asked for a cat. I couldn't keep a cat. But if a cat were here when I came home, well, then, I might have a cat. We'd wait and see.

Time to go to town.

ↄ⁀

I parked my Honda in front of Darvill's bookstore. An Internet search, as well as my own previous explorations, had yielded up not much in the way of cafés, though the bookstore did apparently have a small one. Besides, bookstores are always good places to hang out. They smell nice and attract people who read. It's a fine combination.

It was cozy inside, and not very crowded. Even better, I could smell coffee. I made my way toward the back and found what Jen had promised me. A tiny café indeed; just a counter, with a couch and a few comfy chairs before it. Not even any tables. Hmm. Should I go across the street to the Brown Bear? But that wasn't the sort of place you parked with your laptop for hours. People came in, ate, and left.

The barista caught my eye. "What can I get you?"

"Double mocha, extra hot, no whip," I said, before I could second-guess any further. Fine, I'd try it here for a while.

Mocha in hand, I sat down in one of the comfy chairs and pulled out my laptop. But despite the name, I realized pretty quickly that this was far too awkward. My neck was going to ache from looking down, and I couldn't find an outlet, so what would I do when my battery ran down? Well, I could just drink my coffee and move on…was the Barnacle open yet? I couldn't work in a bar, but maybe I could at least say hi to Jen.

Glancing around the bookstore as I sipped, I noticed a rack of beautiful blank notebooks. Oh, now, there was an idea.

Five minutes later, I opened the notebook across my lap, uncapped a new purple-inked pen, and began writing.

And an hour after that, I looked up, astonished to find all the rest of the seats around me taken, my stone-cold-extra-hot-double-mocha-no-whip on the little coffee table before me, and a dozen or more handwritten pages in the notebook.

Well, that worked just fine. It's harder to delete what's written in pen.

&

From there I hunted up the Island Hoppin' Brewery, on a road out by the island's tiny airport. Was everything tiny on islands in general, or just on *this* island? My dinner on Colin's boat was fast approaching. I had to pick up a growler.

I had the address, but I found the brewery mostly by following little makeshift signs placed strategically along the way. The place itself was in a warehousey-looking building amid a bunch of other warehousey-looking buildings—almost the first non-picturesque thing I'd seen on Orcas Island. Well, other than the sheriff's substation.

I parked in the gravel lot and made my way to the front door, feeling more and more dubious as I went. It looked like the sort of place you'd go to buy bulk animal feed or construction hardware, not beer. But when I pushed open the door and the heady scent of hops met my nose, I knew I was in the right place.

Inside, it was cozy and convivial—not quite as picturesque as the Barnacle, but just as welcoming. A five-seater bar lined one wall, with a few tables taking up the rest of the small room.

The only customers were a young couple in the corner playing cards, half-emptied glasses of beer before them. A somewhat nerdy-looking fellow with big glasses behind the bar looked up as I came in and gave me an appealing smile.

"Hi," I said, sitting on one of the barstools.

"Welcome!" he answered. "What can I get you?"

I felt a blush coming on, not because he was so overtly flirtatious (he was just working, after all), but because apparently my mind was evaluating every man I met for dating potential. Really? This soon?

No way.

I scanned the menu, handwritten in colorful chalk on a big board behind him. "Hmm. I'm looking for a growler, but I don't know of what exactly…"

"What's it for?"

"Dinner at a new friend's house. Good with seafood. He just said light, maybe ale. He said you could help me choose something."

"Dinner with a new friend, hm?" He nodded and turned to study the board behind him. "Well, nothing we have is terribly light, but a lot of it is good with food. Have you tried the Old Madrona?"

I shook my head.

"Or the Elwha Rock IPA?"

"I've never been here before. I haven't tried any of your beers."

"What?" He turned back to face me, tossing his arms in the air in mock exasperation. "That is a terrible thing! We must remedy that at once!"

It wasn't like me to giggle, but I did it, I giggled. "And how shall we do that?"

"A flight, of course," he said at once, pointing to the chalkboard. Ah yes, now I saw that I could sample them all for ten dollars… "A taste of all seven," he went on cheerfully. "Shall I get that going for you?"

I looked around. The place seemed entirely safe. If I drank a little something and my ability to vanish left me, I would be all right.

"Sure, why not?" It was just a taste of each, right?

He pulled out seven small glasses, then began drawing beer into each of them from the many different taps behind the counter, setting each one before me on a numbered coaster as its head settled. "I'll line them up in the recommended order," he said, "but feel free to drink them any way you like."

I watched the growing numbers of glasses. They really weren't all that small, now that they were lined up before me. Well, I didn't have to drink each one down…especially any I didn't particularly like…I was just here to taste, after all. "And then she went out on a strange island and ordered seven beers," I joked, "and no one ever heard from her again…"

He laughed. "Orcas is strange? You're not from here?"

Could he possibly think I was a native? "No, Seattle, most recently. I'm caretaking out in West Sound."

He set the final glass before me with a flourish. "Cool! I'm from Seattle too—moved here last year." Before I could respond, he went on: "And now, from left to right, we have the K-Pod Kolsch, the Old Madrona Imperial Red, the Elwha Rock IPA, the Doe Bay ISA, the Old Salts Brown Ale, the Camano Coffee Porter, and the Yardarm Oatmeal Stout. And Brian."

I followed along, trying to memorize his list. "Excuse me? What's Brian?"

He put his hand out across the bar. "That's me."

"Oh! I'm Cam," I said, as I shook. "Lovely to make your acquaintance, Brian."

He winked behind his nerdy glasses. "Drink up."

☙

I sipped, I sampled, I tasted. I ate some peanuts to sop up the alcohol. I was very, very responsible. But the beer was very, very good.

The tasting room started to fill up—with regulars, I could tell. First the few tables were taken, then every seat at the bar. I ended up moving down to the end so some folks could sit together. The couple playing cards left; four people immediately occupied their table. It got so crowded, you could hardly walk through the room, but Brian flitted about, taking care of everyone easily, comfortably. He reminded me of Jen. Some people are just naturals at food (and drink) service, they make it look easy. Not me. Fortunately, haircuts happened one person at a time.

Except if you were doing color on someone, which had to set for thirty or more minutes; then you could go do a quick cut on someone else. Unless it was time for a break, or something. Would I ever cut hair again? Who did hair on Orcas Island?

So many people here, they *had* to get haircuts. Could I *help*?

Perhaps I was a little tipsy.

Another shift of people beside me, and suddenly the fellow next to me was saying something. To me, I mean. "Excuse me?" I gazed at him, somewhat bleary-eyed. He looked familiar. And he was super cute, with short hair that filled the top of his head with springy curls just begging to be patted. I smiled at him. "I just love your hair."

He blinked, then smiled back. "Why thank you. I hope you've got someone to drive you home, Ms. Tate."

"Home?" I said, most intelligently. Then: "Deputy Rankin! I didn't recognize you without your…" I motioned. "Your clothes." Of course he was wearing clothes. "I mean your uniform." But there was something…different…? "Your *cap.*"

The deputy smiled again. "Off duty. Out of uniform. Cap off. Call me Kip."

"Kip! Is that short for something?"

"Yes." But he didn't elaborate. I started formulating a question, to ask him what it was, then gave up. The idea was just too complicated, and besides, he would tell me if he wanted to.

Wouldn't he? "I'm just here to buy a growler," I said, enunciating very carefully.

"I see."

"And so I'm just—" I waved at the glasses before me (seven of them, and all nearly empty, how did that happen?) "—tasting. To see which growler to buy."

"I *see*." He glanced up at Brian, who nodded from the other end of the bar, still smiling at the folks he was waiting on. See? Look how observant I was, that I could notice such a thing. Just a little tipsy, is all.

"I need to get the best growler, 'cause I'm going to *dinner*. On a *boat*."

"You might do well to have some dinner here, Ms. Tate."

"Oh! I don't mean tonight!" I laughed, putting a hand on his arm. It was very muscular, his arm, and warm, too, there under his flannel shirt. It steadied me.

Hey. Wait. Did he think I was *drunk*?

"I did have some dinner here tonight, though. I mean, I had, uh…" Hadn't I eaten something?

Brian walked over. "Hey, Kip, what'll ya have?"

"Pint of Old Madrona for me, and four deviled eggs and a big glass of water for Ms. Tate here."

"Right-o." Brian pulled Kip's beer and set it in front of him, then turned to fill a glass with water.

"That one's *delicious*," I said, pointing to Kip's tall glass of amber liquid. "I think that's what I'll get for the growler."

"It is good," he said, taking a sip, then setting it down rather obviously out of my reach.

He *did* think I was drunk!

Brian returned with my water. I took a big, grateful sip. Actually, that did taste pretty good too. "Eggs are coming right up," he said, more to the deputy than to me.

"You can clear those," Kip said to him, pointing to my nearly empty beer glasses.

"Hey, so," I started, but then stopped, not sure what I'd been meaning to say.

Really, I had probably had enough beer.

Kip took another swig of his Old Madrona. "So, Ms. Tate—"

"If I'm calling you *Kip*, you call me *Cam*," I interrupted.

He smiled. "All right."

"Oh and hey!" I remembered what I wanted to know. "What did you find out about the passport?"

His smile grew a little faint on his face. "You know I can't tell you. It's an ongoing investigation." He sounded so patient.

"Oh *right*." I smacked my forehead, meaning to make it sort of an in-jest gesture (*jest*-ure! Ha!), but overshooting and kind of hitting a little hard. Ow. I steadied myself on the barstool. "Right." *Be cool, Cam.* "So. Now what shall we talk about?" I gave him a brilliant smile.

"Eat your eggs."

I looked down. A plate of four gorgeous deviled egg halves had appeared in front of me. They were *masterpieces*. And I hadn't even seen Brian bring them! A ninja, that's what he was. A veritable deviled-egg ninja! "Okay!" I picked one up and took a bite. "Yum."

Kip watched me eat all four, or nearly—I was midway through the last one when I suddenly realized maybe I was being rude. "Wait—do you want some?"

He shook his head, smiling. "No, Cam. Those are all for you. Now drink your water."

I obeyed. He was a cop, after all. You do what cops tell you to do.

I set the empty glass back on the bar. Brian appeared and took it away, then brought it back a moment later, full again. The water and the protein in my stomach joined forces and began their work of bringing me back to myself. "Well, I guess I needed that."

Kip smiled. "We all need a little snack now and then. And

those eggs are particularly delicious."

"Delicious. Like your voice. Did you know your voice is delicious? It sounds like a bucket of honey."

"Is that right?" He looked like he might be going to laugh, but for some reason, he didn't. "So tell me more about yourself," Kip said, leaning back and giving me an inviting smile. "Everything, starting from day one."

"You don't *really* want to know all that. You're just trying to keep me here so I'll sober up," I accused.

"That's exactly what I'm trying to do. Though I *am* off duty, and I'd be happy to drive you back out to Massacre Bay if you need a ride."

"Wait, *what?*"

"I said, I'm off duty—"

"No, after that." I was feeling more sober all the time. "Drive me out to where?"

He gave me a bemused look. "Massacre Bay. That's where the Brixton estate is. Where you live? You *do* remember where you live?"

"You are *kidding* me. *Massacre* Bay?"

He shook his head. "Scout's honor. Your place, the Cannon place, and the Fourniers on the other side—that dock you all share, that's the landing at Massacre Bay."

"And that's Skull Island just offshore," Brian put in, now standing before us.

"And Victim Island a little further out," Kip added.

I gaped at them both.

"Ancient history," Kip went on. "Native American thing."

I shook my head. "And no one thinks any of that is…inauspicious?"

Brian laughed. "Just colorful, I think."

"Wow." I started to shake my head again, but that threatened to make the tipsiness return. I sipped more water. "I thought it was West Sound."

"Massacre Bay is part of West Sound, yes," Brian said.

"What an interesting island this is," I said. Wait, did they think I was being judgey? "But I think it's great here," I added, reassuringly. "Everyone's so friendly. And I'm not just saying that because of all the beer."

Kip laughed. "I'm glad to hear that."

"No, seriously: I haven't even been here two weeks, and I've already made more friends than I did in three years in Seattle."

"The Seattle Freeze," Brian put in, now halfway down the bar.

I nodded. "And it's funny—I always thought it was small towns that were supposed to be the insular, hard-to-break-into ones."

"It's a little different in the summertime, in high tourist season," Kip said. "But yes: it is a friendly island."

"Yes. *Friendly*." What a friendly place this was. And here I was making friends! It would be interesting to see it in the summertime. What must it be like, to have your home overrun by strangers for months on end?

I supposed I would see, in time.

Kip was talking again. "Have you met Paige Berry yet?"

"No, but you're the second person to ask me that. Who is she?"

Kip grinned, and traded a look with Brian. "How 'bout I just say 'famous local character' and leave it at that?"

"You people are all so mysterious." I glanced around the tiny, crowded tasting room. "Say, this place doesn't have a bathroom, does it?"

❧

I managed to navigate my way to the ladies' room and back with very little difficulty and a minimum of bumping into other people's chairs. The eggs were definitely helping. When I returned, I settled up with Brian for the flight, struggling with the sense that I was forgetting something. Was it the eggs? No, Kip wasn't letting me pay for the eggs. Not only that, but he insisted on walking me out to my car—or, rather, supervising my walk to the car, from a few steps behind me.

"Should I put my finger to my nose and hop on one foot?" I asked.

"That won't be necessary," he said. "I'm the expert, and unfortunately, you're no good to drive. I'm taking you home." He opened the door to his patrol SUV, which apparently he drove off-duty, too.

Hmph, I thought, feeling quite a bit more sober than I'd been earlier. Yet from somewhere in my brain came a piece of advice from the distant past: *"Never argue with a cop."* I got in—well, I clambered in, the thing sat up high—and he reached over to fasten my seatbelt before he shut my door.

What a nice fellow, I thought. *And what a beautiful, mellifluous voice he has.*

"Did I tell you that you have a mellf—meffle—wonderful voice?"

"You mentioned something like that, yes."

I decided not to talk, since my vocabulary wasn't working. Okay, maybe I wasn't entirely sober. My head felt loose on my neck, like a bobble-head doll. The thought made me giggle, even though I certainly don't giggle, and the giggling made my head fall around even more, but it only bumped the window once.

"Camille? Are you okay over there?"

"Me? Oh, I'm just *fine*. It's so nice of you to drive me home. It's very…friendly. Everyone here has been friendly so far." Well. Weird but friendly.

"I'm glad you're enjoying the hospitality."

"Kip, did *you* grow up here?" I asked, forgetting that I'd just decided not to talk.

"Sort of. My folks moved here when I was in the eighth grade."

"Oh, that's a hard time to move."

He shrugged. "It was; I hated it at first," he admitted. "Thought I'd be gone from here the moment I was old enough. Then I left—went to college in Bellingham—and I hated that too." He grinned at me. "This place gets into your blood, I guess. Even little Bellingham seemed like a crazy metropolis to me. So I was happy to get back."

"I hope I never have to leave."

"Now, why would you have to leave?"

I shrugged, and this time I stayed quiet for the rest of the ride home.

❦

We made it back to the estate without incident. Kip pulled into my usual spot by the edge of the big garage. "Here you are: safe and sound." I realized that my new notebook was still in the backseat of my car, which I'd left parked in the lot back at the brewery. Was that what I had forgotten? I smiled, remembering my super-productive writing session back at the bookstore, but then felt a pang of disappointment. I'd wanted to incorporate those pages into the computer—it wasn't very late, and I wasn't that drunk, was I?

"Here, kitty," I called. As I looked around for the cat, my mind pleasantly distracted by my screenplay, I almost tripped over a big sandstone rock on my front porch, right before the door. "What the...?"

I tried to pick it up, but it was very heavy.

Kip said, "Leave it, Cam." He leaned down to study it. Underneath was a folded-up piece of paper. "Someone left you a note." He tipped up the rock and with the edges of his fingernails, he withdrew the paper. Still dry; it hadn't been here long, then. He handed it over with a frown. Hands trembling and heart pounding, I unfolded the paper, squinting to see the words in the moonlight.

Mind Your Own Damn Business

I was glad I wasn't sober. It was all that kept me from disappearing right in front of Kip.

CHAPTER 10

An hour later, I sat inside the very-locked-up guesthouse with James.

I hadn't needed to agonize over whether or not I should call 911, since Kip was with me when I found the note.

While he waited, I'd disabled the alarms. Then, Kip had put me back in the patrol car, retrieved a flashlight and taken a look around the entire property. High, low, down by the water, in the garages, in every closet and under every bed in both houses. Once he'd satisfied himself that all was clear, he'd come back to the car for me. His flashlight's beam bobbing along the walkway was the most exquisitely welcome sight I'd ever seen.

He'd offered to spend the night, "On a couch, of course." I'd almost let him. But the alcohol was wearing off and I was still so frightened that I knew I'd start to chameleon. So I'd faked a confidence I didn't feel, bade him goodnight after thanking him, and locked myself inside the guesthouse, staring out the window at the path to Lisa Cannon's estate while I sobered up and dealt with the familiar crawl and tingle of my body's desire to erase itself.

Kip had bagged the note and taken it with him. Could you dust paper for fingerprints? I had no idea. I sat with the cat in my lap, wondering who was warning me. Warning me away from what, exactly? From seeing things I'd never intended to? From finding things that didn't belong to me? From being here in the first place?

How was this my *life*? How was this *happening*?

So much for Orcas being friendly and welcoming!

That's not fair, I told myself, as I got up to pace through the little house—cat at my heels—in an effort to calm down. This was an anomaly, a strange…whatever it was. I'd stumbled into some sort of mystery, totally without meaning to. Well, I could go ahead and stumble right back out of it, I decided. From this moment forward, I would absolutely mind my own business, just as the note demanded.

I looked down at my hands, flickering in and out of perception. No. I needed to calm down. I wasn't in danger tonight. Right? You don't leave someone a note telling her to mind her own business, and then come back and attack her before she can start doing that.

Right?

How in the world was I going to be able to sleep?

I picked up James and snuggled him, wishing he'd purr, but even he could feel the tension.

❧

The next morning, I was sitting in the guesthouse kitchen, showered and dressed, my hair in a ponytail and my fears under control. I heard the gate buzzer sound. I only jumped a little. I was tired and just a little hung over, but I thought I looked presentable enough.

Best of all, I was calm.

I opened the door to a grey drizzle, and Kip in his uniform, ready to give me a ride to my car. James darted out around Kip's ankles, apparently not caring about the rain.

"Good morning. How did you sleep?" Kip's voice was warm, reassuring, and his blue eyes hung slightly at half-mast. I noticed curls peeking out from his cap. I vaguely remembered something about his curls.

I hoped I hadn't patted his curls.

"I'm fine, Kip. I slept…a little." I looked out the window. In the morning, with the light grey skies and rolling water and green lawns around me, I felt calm. Yes, indeed, calm. If there was a threat about, I couldn't find it. "Do you want me to make some coffee before we…"

"I have some in the car. I brought some for you, too."

"That's above and beyond, Deputy."

He smiled the smallest smile. "To serve and protect, Cam."

ↄↄ

I watched the bay roll past out the window, sipping my coffee. A double mocha. No whip. Had he done some research on my coffee tastes?

He cleared his throat. "Cam, I'm wondering if you want me to file an official report."

"Last night wasn't official?"

"Well, no, it actually wasn't. I was off duty. And the note… people communicate a lot with notes around here. 'Please cut your grass so the ticks stay under control.' 'Your dog keeps riling my chickens, please tie him up.' I get calls about notes all the time, but we don't usually end up filing reports for those. And it wasn't like that rock came through your window or anything. Not even a threat, really; I mean, I could tell you about some notes that I consider threatening. Yours was mild. But I can file a report if you like."

"That would be, what, the third police report since my arrival." I pressed my hand to my forehead. "Let me think for a second." The note. It wasn't a threat: it was just an instruction. And as he'd pointed out, it hadn't been left inside my house, just on the porch. No one had broken in. Yes, it was beyond the gates; but anyone could have walked through along the water line. I was safe with the doors locked, the alarms armed. "Kip, I don't want to file another report."

"Are you sure?"

"I'm positive."

"If you change your mind, let me know."

"I will." I let out a sigh of relief. I would not be filing another police report this week.

But I had to do something.

಄

"Crap!" I said, as he pulled into the brewery's parking lot. "I forgot to buy the growler!"

Kip parked next to my car and turned to look at me. "You don't think you had quite enough beer last night, Ms. Tate?"

"No—for the dinner. With…a friend. That's why I was here. I told you."

He nodded, with the ghost of a smile. "You may have mentioned something of the sort. Well, you'll have to come back later; they don't open till noon."

"Ah. Well, thank you for the ride. Both rides." I gave him a sheepish grin.

"My pleasure."

I formed a plan as I drove back to the house. It was about connections.

I would make more connections.

I was already making friends. Just the beginnings of friendship with Colin and Jen, and with Lisa Cannon, but they were there. That was unlike me, and therefore probably a good idea as opposed to a bad idea. Most of my ideas about how to handle life were bad, especially in retrospect. But deepening connections, building a community; that was so not-Camille-like that it had to be a good idea.

I made another decision. I'd told Jen most everything, but now I'd also let Colin know more about what was going on. Just the vague outlines—not hamper any "ongoing investigations" or anything. Just…let them know to be on the lookout in case more weird things happened to me. Or near me. I'd probably told Jen too much already. I'd have to tell her to stop investigating!

And beyond that?

I would work on my screenplay, or stage play, or whatever it wanted to be, and take a chance on showing it to Lisa Cannon. That would bring me even further in to this place, these people. And I would keep in closer touch with my family. Memories of my phone call with Mom last week still brought a pang of guilt to my heart. I'd spent too long shutting people out, keeping my boundaries impossibly high. Mom was very patient.

Speaking of Mom, were they actually going to come out for Thanksgiving? I realized I hadn't heard back about that, and I really needed to know.

I parked in the driveway and got out my phone and dialed her number.

"Oh, Camille, love—I was about to call you," she said, delight in her voice.

I smiled. "But I beat you to it."

"I'll bet you're wondering about Thanksgiving."

"I am indeed."

"Well, it's awfully far, and it's a particularly busy time for your father's work, and I see the ferries only run a few times a day, and you need reservations…"

I sighed, biting back unexpectedly sharp disappointment. Well, it had been a nice idea. "I understand—"

"…but we were thinking we could come out on Wednesday evening, and leave Saturday. Does that work?"

"I…what? You *can* come?"

She chuckled. "Yes, Camille, we would love to come and see your new home. An island sounds so exciting! I only wish your brother could be there."

"Me too." I thought sadly about my brother for a moment.

Why did he have to work so far away? "But, wow, Mom!" My brain was still trying to shift gears. "This will be so great!"

"We do care about you, my dear," she chided, gently. "We always have, from your first night in our home."

I shivered involuntarily. We didn't speak of that night often—I never brought it up; Mom only did when she wanted to make a point. "And I appreciate that, honest," I said. "I love you too." *You saved my life*, I added silently.

There was a brief pause, as we both reflected on times best forgotten. Then she asked, "Are you going to make a turkey?"

"Well, I *could*."

"You could?"

"Sure. I mean, just because I never *have*..."

Her peals of laughter echoed right through me, filling my heart.

We talked a few minutes longer, discussing my thoughts on the menu, what they could bring, what they could help with. I told them to be sure to pack warm clothes and hiking shoes. It was in their company that I'd seen so many of those CCC projects, and I couldn't wait to show them the tower.

When we hung up, I sat back, filled with the happy glow of having people out there who cared about me. No matter how much of a weirdo I was, there were people who accepted me.

Well, as much as they knew of me, anyway.

I was comforted by the imminent arrival of my family, such as it was. It would give me some of my own business to mind.

❧

My comfort was short-lived. Underneath all my "calm" bravado, I was officially freaked out.

Despite all the brilliant notes in purple ink that filled all those pages of my new notebook, I spent the afternoon feeling cross and dissatisfied, tapping ineffectually at my manuscript. James took breaks from licking his whiskers to watch me, the white tip of his tail wriggling in curiosity.

I closed the computer and stood up. "James? We need a break." I might have had a creepy note incident and a dismal writing day, but I could work on my resolution to form connections. I would walk over to Lisa's for happy hour.

I opened the door and nearly tripped over a case of canned cat food that was sitting on the porch. I inspected it carefully for a threatening note, and found none.

"You could have KNOCKED," I called into the trees.

To Sheila, because of course only Sheila would know I needed cat food. Had she left the zucchini? The coffee? The note?

Would the same person who'd left that note leave me cat food?

I stashed the cans on the counter and set off down the path. James came with me part of the way, then scampered off to hunt down a mouse, or a leaf, or an ant.

❧

This time, I wasn't the only guest. I could hear from the front door that at least several people were there, in animated conversation in the huge living room. Lisa was gracious as always, dressed in a simple black cotton dress that, on her, looked opera-worthy. "Cam!" she cried, delighted. "Come in! Finally, you get to meet some more of the gang."

She led me down the few steps into the sunken living room. "Our writer has arrived." A writer? I was a caretaker *née* hairdresser. I felt a blush starting, and wanted to blurt out something dismissive and self-effacing. As if she sensed where I was going, Lisa waved a hand and stopped me. "Cam, meet the troupe. At least some of them! Petey, Charles, Rebecca, Glory—this is Camille Tate." Hm. No Gregory.

The actors all stopped chattering and came to shake my hand, welcoming me with varying degrees of warmth. I fielded introductions and smiled and said polite things, all the while scrutinizing both men, trying to figure out if one of them could have been "Gregory". I couldn't really tell. He had had a ball cap low over his face at first, and I'd been in a state of panic.

Was "Gregory" a character name, or a real name?

It had to be real; the boat was registered to Gregory Baines.

Enough, enough, I told myself. There was no danger here; it was safe to let down my guard. I took a glass of wine and a piece of cheese. The actors, having done their best to charm me, resumed their talk about something that had happened during the day's rehearsal. Though they did not obviously exclude me, they had no need to include me in their specialized conversation.

I didn't have anything to contribute. Like back when Kevin and his foodie friends would gather for potluck. Each speaking with some inborn authority about the flavors and notes and hints and aromatic qualities of each bite of food on the table. And me, just chewing.

Lisa stepped down from the kitchen with a fresh platter of sliced pineapple and huge purple grapes, set it on the coffee table, and came to stand beside me. "They never stop talking shop," she said with a smile.

"No, I guess not."

"Here, sit and talk with me." She took a seat on the couch and patted the cushion next to her. Grateful, I sat down and took a handful of grapes. "How's the writing going?" she asked.

"Ugh, don't ask."

Lisa laughed. "Oh, I'm sorry! I know better, I work with creative types. I hereby give you permission to tell me to shut up if I ever ask again."

"No, it's not a problem," I assured her. "It's just that some days, it goes better than others."

"Of course it does. So, let's see, what else can I ask you? How are you settling in?"

Since she had just given me the perfect opening, I went for it. "Pretty well—I'm meeting nice people, and the island is just gorgeous."

"Yes. Orcas is a truly amazing place."

"I don't see why anyone would ever want to leave here." Did I sound gushing? Well, I meant it—it was truly spectacular.

"Young people seem to." She met my eyes. "That includes you, young lady; you may find our lack of excitement, well, a little dull over time."

Oh, I don't know, seems like I've already found plenty of excitement. "I'm not young; I'm twenty-seven," I protested.

Lisa just laughed and shook her head. "My point exactly. Young."

"Well, I'm older than the last caretaker."

"At the Brixtons'?" She tipped her head slightly, giving me a quizzical look. "What was her name again?"

"Megan."

"That's right. Megan. I'm better with numbers than names."

"And you didn't know her well?"

"She wasn't there for long." She put a grape in her mouth and bit. She chewed and swallowed before answering. "We met, and I gave her my phone number, like you do with neighbors. I didn't invite her to happy hours. She was *very* young, if you know what I mean. You may be all of twenty-seven, but you're rather older than your years—in a good way. I don't think I could have sat and had a comfortable conversation with Megan like I do with you."

"So she wasn't part of your troupe or anything?"

"Oh, gosh, no! What gave you that idea?"

I liked Lisa, and I even thought I could trust her, but I didn't want to talk about the note. "Do you know exactly why she left?"

Lisa shrugged. "Like I said, island life is not for everyone. I assumed she went stir-crazy, and wanted to go back to a livelier place. She did leave right after we had our first snow of the winter."

"Oh?" I hadn't known that. "Does it snow a lot here?"

"Not as much as at higher elevations, but we get at least a dusting several times a winter. Sometimes more. I think it's beautiful, myself."

"Me too." How much to tell her? "I found…some things of hers, that she left behind. But the Brixtons don't know how to get hold of her. Which seems weird to me."

Lisa shook her head. "I'm not sure she was entirely all together. You know, up here." She tapped her forehead with a slender hand. "I would hear things, sometimes—at first it sounded like a very loud television show, and then I thought she was arguing with someone. But I listened, and I would only hear one voice." She held my gaze. "I eventually began to suspect she was arguing with *herself.* I wouldn't be surprised if her parents came and fetched her away and sent her somewhere."

"Oh." And that might also explain leaving the passport behind, and the kitten, if she'd been taken away, rather than leaving of her own free will.

What a terrible thought.

Lisa nodded. "I do get the impression that the Brixtons hired her rather quickly, when JoJo decided to move away." She gave me a gentle smile. "Diana Brixton is not one for deep deliberations or for doing a lot of research before she acts. Didn't you tell me she'd hired you on the spur of the moment?"

"Well, yes, but I've been doing her hair for a few years." Lisa had a point, though. This had all happened pretty fast. Crazy fast. I leaned back and took another bunch of grapes. They were distracting in their delicious magnificence. I wondered how much they'd cost. I wondered if they came from special vines that only wealthy people had access to. I wondered if she had an artisanal grape-growing friend. Maybe the same guy who made the wine. He probably had them flown here on private charter swans equipped with mink-lined baskets strapped to their backs with golden chains wrought by faeries.

Enough distraction. And enough grapes.

"Other than that, things are going well for you? You mentioned meeting interesting people?" Lisa's grey eyes had a glimmer that said she knew something she wasn't saying. How small-town was this island, anyway?

"Yes—Jen Darling, who delivers for all the shipping services and is a bartender at night; and another bartender, at the brewery; and then a…guy named Colin. Do you know him?"

"Colin. Is he that devastatingly handsome boat-builder or something like that?"

"That's him. In fact, he invited me to have dinner on his boat tomorrow."

Lisa looked delighted, leaning forward. "A dinner date on a boat with that exceptionally good-looking ruffian. How exciting!"

I shook my head. "It's just as friends. I'm, well, it's too soon. You know."

Lisa's expression made it clear that she didn't believe me. "Camille, just go with your feelings—trust yourself. If it's too soon, you will know that, and step away. If it's not—let it happen. No one is out here keeping score." She patted her own chest. "*In here* is where the truth lies. For each and every one of us."

I nodded and gave her a helpless smile. She was just so *wise*, even when she was dead wrong. Nothing was going to happen between me and Colin. When it came to romance, I just wanted to be left alone. But I wasn't in the mood to explain or defend myself. "I'm sure you're right—it's an adjustment, all of this. I sometimes wonder if it was a good idea, moving to a place so quiet, so remote. But at least it gives me space to think."

She laughed, warm and gentle. "Well, you're a writer: thinking is your bread and butter. And if you get too bored, remember my offer. I'll keep you busy."

The crowd in the middle of the room—yes, four people can be a crowd, when they're that animated—suddenly burst into a great gust of raucous laughter. Lisa turned to look at them, as did I.

But I was more interested in Sheila. She'd slipped into the

room from the hallway sometime in the last few minutes, and now leaned against the wall on the other side of the living room, sipping a Mike's Hard Lemonade and glaring at the actors. She looked to be more uncomfortable than I was with those actors. Didn't she know them, and run lines and all with them?

I decided to clear up one mystery. While Lisa got up to join the conversation with her actors, I made my way across the room to Sheila.

"I wanted to say thanks."

She set her mouth in a thin line and glared at me.

"For the food. I hadn't realized how much a growing…"

She shook her head ever-so-slightly, and her eyes rolled in unmistakable warning.

I made my exit soon thereafter, before my skin could start tingling.

❧

I didn't hear any footsteps following me home, which was a relief. I could think, rather than listen and panic. As I walked, I made a mental list of what I knew.

Megan, my predecessor, was gone, and no one knew why she left or where she went. She was young, spring-break young. And flighty.

She might have been flighty and young and mentally unbalanced, but that only made me more concerned about her whereabouts, not less.

Someone didn't want me to know the truth about Megan. Whoever it was, he or she left that note.

Sheila was no actor. And neither was Megan.

And James, my little orange leaf-hunter, was some kind of secret weapon.

Sheila had to have been the one who had left the note. Was she behind Megan's mysterious disappearance? If so, why? Or was she just crazy? She sure seemed angry all the time. Even gentle, cheerful Lisa had sounded testy when she talked about her.

But angry wasn't crazy. Or not necessarily, at least.

Should I talk to Kip about this—off the clock, not calling 911?

But what did I have to say, exactly? "The neighbor lady's weird personal assistant gave me a kitten." Okay, he'd been with me when we'd found the note on the doorstep. And that was definitely something. So he knew I wasn't making all this up, but really, a kitten?

What else could I report to Kip? The menacing appearance of suspicious out-of-season zucchini on my doorstep? Oh, and the mysterious coffee beans.

I just hated looking stupid, looking like a foolish alarmist who thought everything that happened was sinister and threatening. Except, a note under a rock on my very doorstep? Telling me to mind my own business? That actually was sinister and threatening. Enough that Kip had gone over the entire property before he finally agreed to leave.

And yet he'd sort of shrugged off the note, even though he'd taken it with him. *"Neighbors leave notes all the time here."*

Really?

I was so good at doubting myself.

I emerged from the pathway onto the Brixtons' estate, walked quietly back around the house and garage to the guesthouse, and approached it slowly, looking all around for signs of…anything. The whole place was surrounded by woods—well, where it wasn't abutting the water. The lapping water of Massacre Bay.

It had seemed so peaceful before. Now it seemed eerie. Isolated, hidden…dangerous?

I tiptoed to my car and peered inside. It looked untouched. I made it up to my front porch. No rock, no note, no coffee, no vegetables. James was nowhere in sight. I unlocked the door and let myself in, snapping on the lights.

Everything seemed fine. I walked through the whole house, looking in every room, but no one was here, nothing was disturbed. I stopped myself before I could look through all the closets and under the beds. That was just giving in to nerves.

I put the kettle on for tea, opened a can of food and dumped it in a bowl on the counter. I opened the back door to let out a "Here kitty, kitty," but before I could, James came running in on his long wild-kitten legs and jumped up on the counter to help himself.

"I don't think you're supposed to be up there," I told him. He ignored me and applied himself to his dinner.

I closed the door and went to light a fire. I decided that James had the right idea. Once I got some dinner in me, and made the place warm and light, it would feel so much more safe and cozy. Then I could spend what was left of the evening writing.

Today's progress had been sub-optimal indeed.

❧

The next morning, Jen Darling swung by again while she was out on her rounds. Same black slicker, and this time she carried a little backpack, which she opened with a flourish. "I have a delivery for you."

True to her word, she had a big ziploc bag stuffed with zucchini-pecan muffins. "Oh, my goodness," I exclaimed as I opened the bag and the aroma wafted out. Once I had us settled at the kitchen table with tea and two plump, heated muffins slathered with butter, I said, "Thank goodness you're here. I'm totally stuck in scene two. Now I can ignore it."

She made a grab for her little backpack and stood up. "Omygosh! You were writing! I'm leaving at once!" Then she ruined the effect by bursting into laughter.

"Sit down, sit down." I patted her chair; she complied. "Honestly," I said with a sigh, "I don't know how real writers do it."

"You're a real writer!"

"Oh, I am not—I'm just trying."

"If you write, you're a real writer. Did you try working in

town?"

"I did, at the bookstore. They didn't have actual tables, though; I handwrote on my lap."

She nodded. "You should try Teezer's. They have tables. And they have amazing cookies."

I patted my belly. "Oh, that's *just* what I need."

"Camille Tate! You are gorgeous and voluptuous!"

"And becoming more so every day, with these bakeries. Not to mention these amazing muffins." We grinned at each other a moment as I pondered the fact that I was discussing my weight with someone I hardly knew.

"Wait, is that another one?" Jen was frowning at my second huge zucchini, which lay in green repose on the counter. "You have *another* zucchini?"

"Yes. But don't worry, you don't have to make me more muffins. I'm going to figure out something else to do with it. I'm almost out of baby bok choy, so...I'm not much of a cook."

"Well, I heard you're having dinner with Colin on the boat tonight. You'll eat well there." Jen actually raised her eyebrows when she said that.

I rolled my eyes. "Yes. I'm having dinner with Colin on his boat—in fact, I have to get into town this afternoon and pick up a growler."

"Yum." She growled, grinning. "Sexy."

"Oh, please. This evening has about as many romantic possibilities as a dental appointment. I'm not in any shape for dating."

Jen nodded. "That's probably for the best, because neither is he. He's still completely torn up over Beth." She shrugged. "I mean, I liked Beth fine, but they were never really convincing to me. But he's devastated."

"He said they grew up here together?"

"We all did. And with so few people here, couples happen like that. You get together in the fifth grade and end up married somehow. Beth was always too ambitious for that to happen, though. Beth was always going places."

I found myself oddly interested in whatever details Jen could give me about Beth. "So, she's ambitious."

"Very. And she's nice, too, don't get me wrong. But—well, it's good she's gone out into the real world. She was always looking for something that she was never going to find here."

"The 'real world.' Colin called it 'America.'"

Jen raised an amused eyebrow. "I can't believe he said that to an *American*. He must really like you." I shrugged. "So, dinner on the boat—what are you going to wear?"

"It doesn't matter! It's not a date!" I stuffed my mouth with another generous bite of zucchini muffin as she laughed.

"Okay, so Colin's not your type. Who else can we find for you?"

My cheeks warmed as I immediately thought of Kip. I mean Deputy Rankin. Flustered by this, and by my contradictory resolves to both mind my own business and make closer connections with folks here, I blurted out, "We have to stop investigating things."

Jen stared at me, obviously thrown by the sudden subject change. "What?"

"I found a note. The other night. Warning me." As she frowned, I went on. "But Deputy Rankin was here, he took it away. After searching the whole property."

"Rankin? He was here?"

"I had too much to drink and he gave me a ride home. He was a perfect gentleman."

"Of course he was." She smiled with just a shade of rue. "He's always a perfect gentleman. Not very imaginative, and he *loves loves loves* his rules. But he's a good egg."

Egg. He'd bought me eggs. And I'd patted his hair. Or thought about it; I wasn't sure. Certainly I'd blathered about it. "He seems nice," I said. "He rescued me from the after-effects of a sample flight of beer at Island Hoppin'."

"He's good about that. We have next to no DUIs around here,

thanks to his unofficial taxi system. I mean it, he's a good one. And he was with you when you found the note?"

"He was, and he didn't think I needed to report it."

Jen nodded. "I'd trust his judgment. You should see the notes people leave around here. They leave me a one-page note telling me where to hide their packages, and pin it right up where a thief could read it." We both laughed. "But who do you think left your note? Do you think it was from that grumpy Sheila character?"

"I don't think so. Because she brought me over a kitten."

"A kitten?" James was back snoozing on my bed; she hadn't seen him yet.

"A kitten. And a case of cat food."

"She brought you a *kitten*?"

"Yes. It used to be Megan's. So why would Sheila bring me a kitten and then tell me to mind my own business?" I shrugged. "But I'm not at all clear why—I mean, what's the problem? How am I *not* minding my own business here? I'm just living, writing, meeting folks. Caretaking. Eating zucchini muffins."

"And maybe going to the cops a couple of times, including your first day here, accusing your neighbor of murder."

I gave her a helpless look. "Well, that was a mistake, obviously."

"And maybe nosing around on the neighbor's dock."

"Hey, that was *your* idea! Nobody's leaving you notes!"

She laughed. "Not like that, no."

"And then I just turned in something that was lost. What would *you* do if you found a passport?"

Jen put her hands up in mock-surrender. "Hey, I'm not criticizing. I'm just trying to see it from—whoever's—point of view. I actually agree with you." Now she grinned. "It does make me super intrigued, though." She reached into her backpack and pulled out some folded papers. "Which reminds me, since you mention the neighbor's dock: it's time to put these back."

"Oh great. That's minding my business for *sure*."

Jen rolled her eyes. "Oh, come on. Maybe next time, I'll get the note and need rescuing from the valiant Deputy Kip."

"I did a Google search on Gregory Baines, but I didn't find anything."

"That's because you're not nearly as good at snooping as I am." She gave a coy smile.

I leaned forward. "What did you find?"

She sat back with a look of satisfaction. "He has a commercial fishing license. He even appeared on two seasons of *Savage Tides*."

"What in the world is *Savage Tides*?"

Jen gave me an incredulous look. "Do you watch no TV at all? It's that show about fishing in Alaska."

Hm. Maybe he was an actor of sorts.

"Enough talk—let's do this!" And with a flash of red curls and shiny black slicker, she was out the back door of the guesthouse and headed for Massacre Bay.

I pulled on my red boots, grabbed one of my Nordic wonder-sweaters, and practically ran to catch up with her.

ↄↄ

"Hurry, okay?"

"No one can see us, Cam."

The dingy little craft was right where we'd left it, bobbing on water that looked a little grey, since the day was overcast. My job was lookout, and Jen's job was to put back the paperwork she never should have taken in the first place. My heart was hammering and I was afraid of being afraid, afraid of the slight trickle of fear that set my skin to tingling. I didn't want to vanish. I concentrated on breathing, on the lumpy, grey undersides of the clouds, on the toes of my boots and the fact that my fingernails needed cutting.

What was taking her so long?

Her curls appeared, and the relief that flooded my body settled my skin immediately. She gave me a wink that let me know just how much she actually enjoyed the intrigue and sneaking. I took a few deep breaths and we turned back to walk along the shore.

"You were actually in and out of there pretty fast."

"I should have been an international jewel thief, I guess. But I'm just an Orcas Island two-jobber. And now I have to go make some real deliveries."

I looked up at the lifting clouds, which were fraying like an old towel, letting the sun glint through. "It's getting pretty. You want to take a walk before you go? Then I'll follow you into town."

"Another day—I really do have to run. Is the house open? My backpack's in there."

"It's open." I realized that I kept forgetting to lock the doors when I left the house. With the gates and all, it seemed so redundant, despite the note.

"Are you sure you don't want me to do some more zucchini magic? No muffins, I promise. I have so many things to do with zucchini that are not muffins."

I nearly blushed. "Oh, would you?"

She tossed those red curls in amusement. "Abracadabra." She sprinted up the lawn to the house, her slicker shining, her hair bobbing.

Me, I decided to wander along the waters of the Straits of Juan de Fuca. In the *opposite* direction of the Cannon estate. The clouds were breaking up, the air smelled so clean and fresh, and my boots only slipped a little as I picked my way from grass to rock to grass again, admiring the water.

I felt better with the papers back in the boat. I had to admit that Jen and I made a good team. I wondered about everything, turned it over in my mind, tried to find patterns and reasons and connections, but Jen took action. Between the two of us, we had "all the bases covered," as my foster dad liked to say. Dad and his baseball metaphors. The thought made me smile, looking forward to his visit at Thanksgiving.

I'd never walked this far up the bay. I wondered which of the little islands in the channel belonged to America, and which belonged to Canada. This was the kind of arcane maritime knowledge that was impossible for me, someone who'd been here about two weeks, to know.

But maybe. In time. If I stayed, and got to know these waters. After all, I was making friends with a guy who had a boat. Certainly Colin would take me to that island in the distance. It was such a perfect little green hummock, it looked like it could roll over. Like a seal.

Orcas shoreline was on the rugged side. I'd walked maybe a half-mile when the low, rocky bluff receded, leaving a stretch of stony beach I could walk on. If it ever got warm enough to swim in these northern waters, I decided this would be the place, even with the rocks underfoot and the driftwood deposited here and there. Driftwood always reminded me of beach fires and a gallery show that Kevin had catered in Seattle. I'd come along to hand out delicious appetizers, and had seen the show as I wielded my tray. The artist, a woman from California, gathered driftwood and used it to make sculptures of muses, mothers, mermaids. Always women. Looking at the heaps of wood on the rocky shore, I had to agree with the artist that the worn, sinuous shapes lent themselves to the female form. But it was all so grey. Weren't women more colorful?

I approached a particularly tall tangle that mostly blocked the beach. I wondered if this was a sign: should I scramble over and keep going, or head back to the house and make my run into town? There was a piece of wood in there of a shape so completely feminine, I almost wished I had that California artist's name. She would have hardly had to shape this one at all. The smooth, tapering back, the narrow waist, the unmistakable rise of a woman's hip. It was uncanny. I had to investigate.

I stepped closer, wondering if I could disentangle this log from the others. A branch lay up over the head, amazing me with how much it resembled an arm, resting in a delicate way on dark, shining seaweed that looked exactly like wet hair. It was so beautiful and so very, very strange, like a mermaid had washed up on Orcas Island.

Three more steps, and I understood why that smooth piece of driftwood looked so much like a woman.

Because it was a woman.

A woman's body, grey with death, washed up on the beach of Massacre Bay.

ℭ

My invisibility was swift, profound, and paralyzing. I couldn't move or speak or scream or call for help. I could only wait, stunned and terrified, while my skin crawled with the pricking, stinging chameleon reaction that hid me from outside perception. I didn't want to hide. While I waited, I stared at the grey, battered body of the woman in the wood. I wanted to help whoever that was, but she was past anyone's help. She was not alive, I told myself. She was just one part of a washed-up, waterlogged tangle. Whatever had happened to her, she couldn't feel it anymore. She was gone.

Finally, I began to shiver. To shiver, and to move. To stumble back, tripping as I tried to run, finally reaching the guesthouse, the door, my cell phone, the dispatcher.

Kip Rankin arrived first, lights and sirens blaring. "Are you all right?"

I nodded yes, then shook my head no. I was not all right.

"Camille, can you lead me there?" he asked, and I nodded again. I would lead him there, but I was terrified that I'd vanish. What if I vanished?

Still, whoever that was, she needed my help. Even though she was dead.

Kip followed me down to the water and up the bay, speaking on his handheld radio all the while. As we walked, I could see the lights of a Coast Guard cutter just off the coast. Thanks to Kip's coordinates, they arrived at the tangle of driftwood almost as soon as we did.

"There," I said, pointing. "There she is."

"I see her." Kip took one minute to remove his cap and place it over his heart. Then, he was all business. I watched as long as I could, which was just as long as it took for the Coast Guard medic to check for a pulse. I turned away when it appeared they were going to roll her over. I just couldn't bear to see that, to see her face. I wasn't afraid of what the sea and death might have done to her. I was more afraid that she'd look fine, that she'd look like someone sleeping. Like someone I knew, even.

I stared out at the water, feeling numb.

At least this time, no one tried to tell me that what I'd seen wasn't real.

CHAPTER 11

I don't even exactly remember how I got back to the guest-house after that. Did I walk? Alone, or did Kip escort me? I know I went right to bed, because I woke up there, confused and disoriented, in the pre-dawn dark. Five-in-the-morning dark. My clothes and boots and cell phone lay in a heap on the bedroom floor where I must have dropped them before collapsing into oblivion. James snuggled against my hip, fast asleep.

I pushed myself up to sit on the edge of the bed, where I paused a moment, blinking away the cobwebs. Remembering. A dead woman, washed up on the beach. A young woman. So I'd taken Deputy Kip to the body, answered a few questions, come back here and hit the bed and slept straight through, late afternoon till morning. A different way of vanishing? At least sleep was something other people did. I was hit with a wave of longing for Kevin; Kevin, the man who'd slept beside me for so long, the man who could make me feel better. But Kevin was gone, and the day was here, and it looked like a grey and grim one out there.

Grey. Grim.

I shivered again, thinking of it, then quickly got up and pulled on yesterday's clothes. James slept through it all. Well, he was a growing boy. Cup of exquisite mystery coffee in hand (because if I deserved coddling on any day, it was this day), I went to my office and booted up my computer.

My email loaded; I startled at the first subject line to pop up: WE NEED TO TALK.

It was from Jen. I clicked to open the message, but there was none—just a link to the *Orcas Daily News & Notes* online newspaper.

Which led straight to an article about a local resident finding a body on the beach. The article didn't name me, or the victim, but there were enough identifying details—"...caretaker at a West Sound estate...recently arrived on the island..."—that anyone who knew anything at all would figure out I was the one who'd found it. Who had written this? I didn't remember any reporters on the beach.

I do NOT have it in me to resist Jen right now, I thought. I imagined her interrogation. What would I even say? Yikes, she could have been with me when I'd found it, if she hadn't had to get back to work. Would that have been better, or worse? Definitely worse. I'd vanished hard, and instantly. There would have been no way to finesse that with her.

Anyway, it was too early to call or text anyone, so I just answered the email: *I most definitely cannot talk about any of this with you. Call me when you get up, but understand that I can't talk about ANYTHING.* I'd deal with her when I had to.

❧

I decided that part of my shaking was hunger. I didn't remember eating much the day before. After a second cup of coffee, one of Jen's zucchini muffins and some scrambled eggs, I remembered something else about the night before.

I'd had plans.

"Oh, CRAP," I said aloud. I'd completely blown off Colin's dinner on his boat. And he must be pissed. He hadn't called or texted or anything.

If he'd read the news, wouldn't he have texted?

"Crap!" I said again, getting up from the table and pacing around the kitchen. What must he be thinking? He knew I wasn't ready to start another romance—neither was he. But we'd agreed to be friends. He must think I was a total jerk. I had to talk to him, but not only was I not in the mood to talk about what I'd found, I had been instructed not to. Kip had explained that his office had to control the flow of information to the public. And that was just fine by me, because the last thing I wanted to do was talk about her.

That smooth, grey back. That wet hair. I was shivering, my skin tingling.

Enough, enough. Think about other things, Cam. It was about seven. Too early to call someone who lived on the water? I didn't know, but I'd risk it.

His phone went straight to voicemail. I didn't leave a message. Some apologies should be made in real time.

◈

Jen finally texted a little after ten. *Busy day, come see me at Barnacle @ noon?*

Bar is open that early? I texted back.

Special event.

As I was typing an answer, my cell phone rang: 'SJCSD' was the caller ID, and the number was local. "Hello?" Had I put this number in my phone?

"Cam, how are you doing this morning?" Kip's golden voice.

I sighed, unaccountably relieved to hear such friendliness and concern. "I don't know," I said. "A little bleary—I must have slept fourteen hours. And I don't remember getting home. Did you get me back here?"

He sounded so sympathetic. "I did, and I tucked you into bed. You were almost in shock. I'm glad you slept."

"Like crazy." I shook my head. "I don't know how that happened." Now that he mentioned it, I did sort of remember being guided here. Did he undress me? Cripes.

He paused a moment. "So, are you feeling up to coming in to the station this afternoon? We have a few more things we need to ask you."

"And then I'll be done?" I wanted to be done.

"I hope so."

"I hope so, too. When?"

"Any time after about two. But call first."

"I will. And have you figured out who it is?"

A small sigh. "I'll tell you what I can when you're here."

After we'd hung up, I finished texting Jen. *I'll be in around 1, gotta go see the cops at 2.*

So it was you who found it????

I thought for a moment about lying, but decided it was pointless. *You guessed it.*

James wandered into the room, stretching his long legs and blinking up at me. And at seeing his little orange self, I felt a glimmer of cheer. Just a glimmer, but that and this amazing coffee would get me through the day. "At least I didn't sleep as long as a *cat*," I said to him. "I hope all these phone calls and texts didn't interrupt your beauty rest, Mr. Super Secret Bodyguard."

"Meow," he said, most eloquently, which I took to mean *Where is breakfast?* and responded accordingly.

❧

The Barnacle was a crazy bustle of activity, especially considering there were no customers. "What's going on?" I asked Jen, when she spotted me and came over.

"We're catering a wedding—well, the booze part, anyway. Have a seat. I've got maybe five minutes."

We sat at a table in the front window. Behind the bar, several young people in crisp white shirts and black pants packed boxes full of bottles and glasses, calling out instructions and orders, squeezing to push past one another in the tiny space. A young woman glanced over at me, her eyes widening a bit. Then she whispered to the fellow standing next to her, wiping wine glasses with a bar towel, whereupon he glanced at me.

So, everyone knew.

I cringed, and looked back at Jen. "Big wedding?"

"Yeah." She pushed an escaped curl out of her face. "Want a drink?"

"Um, no thanks." Should I, though? Before going and talking to Kip? No. That wouldn't be scary. He just had more questions. I could do this.

Was *everyone* talking about me?

"You look horrible."

"I feel worse."

"So." She leaned in, looking scandalized, yet still intrigued. "You can tell me a little, can't you?"

"You know I can't." I shivered, wishing for that drink after all. "It was awful. I thought it was a piece of driftwood. So I got closer and...it wasn't." My skin tingled. I took a deep breath.

"Do they know who it was?"

"If they do, they haven't told me."

"Unreal." She shook her head. Behind her, from the bar, someone called out "Jen? Are we bringing this whole case of schnapps?"

"Yes!" she called back. "And the peach mix as well—the box under that." She looked at me and sighed. "Sorry."

"That's all right. I don't have much time either." I frowned. "I blew off Colin last night—I didn't mean to, but I just went home after it all and zonked out. And now I can't get hold of him."

"Ohhhh," she said. "*That's* what that was."

"What?"

She gave a rueful smile. "Try the Lower Tavern. You will want to talk to him. He'll understand."

"He's pissed, isn't he?"

"He'll understand," she repeated. "Just tell him."

"How do *you* know but he doesn't?"

"'Cause he's a guy. Everyone knows, who's paying any attention at all. He's just not listening. He's busy feeling stood up."

I laughed. "Oh."

"Hey Jen!" called out another woman from behind the bar.

Jen rose to her feet. "Listen—let's talk later. I gotta get back to this."

"Sure."

She reached out and gave me a short hug, which I actually appreciated. I wanted a hug, but from Kevin. Pathetic? Yes. But I missed him more than ever.

I slipped out of the Barnacle and walked down Prune Alley past the grocery store, approaching the dive bar. I'd never been inside the Lower Tavern before. The nachos-and-beer smell was just as potent as ever. If not for the aroma, and the fact that the door was ajar, I'd have thought the place was closed. It was that dark inside.

Or maybe it was just tinted windows? I opened the door more widely—nope, just dark in here. As my eyes adjusted to the gloom, I made out a scattering of tables, captain's chairs, a long bar against the far wall. A *crack* of a cue stick against a ball indicated a pool table. This place was as huge and charmless as the Barnacle was tiny and adorable.

"Help you?" A young woman was behind the bar, straight blond hair pulled back in a ponytail.

"I'm…looking for someone?" I managed, trying to smile at her and search the room at the same time. A weathered old man sat at the end of the bar like a movie prop, complete with empty shot glass and can of 3.2 before him. Three guys who must barely be twenty-one sat at one of the tables drinking Budweiser from cans. I heard another *crack* of the pool cue, and then a very familiar laugh. "Oh—he's here."

She shrugged and went back to watching a game show on the TV behind the bar.

My boots stuck to the floor a little, making little squeaky-sticky sounds as I walked up to the pool table.

Colin was indeed there, long pool cue in hand, leaning over the table. Three other guys were with him, all in faded blue jeans and work boots. Flannel shirts and hooded sweatshirts completed the dress code. Colin glanced up, then looked pointedly back down at the table, lining up his shot.

I waited till he'd made it—sinking the three into a corner pocket—before speaking. "Colin, I'm so sorry about last night."

One of the other guys snickered softly, but Colin gave him a dirty look. "Shut up, Gus," he said, with rough affection, and now the other guys laughed as well. I don't want to say they were a seedy-looking bunch, because Colin fit right in with them. Like he belonged. Which was a puzzle in itself…but then, they were clearly all longtime locals. And then I remembered Colin's small awkwardness in the precious little Barnacle bar, on our first not-date. Of course. *Here* he was a regular, not that trendy, pretty-much-touristy place.

Colin looked back at me. "Decided not to risk it after all?"

"It's not that. I…I don't know if you heard about the body, a dead body, on the beach…"

Four pairs of eyes widened; four male bodies leapt into various forms of action. Within a minute, I found myself seated at a table, with a bottle of Heineken before me. *Guess I get that drink after all*, I thought.

"I thought you looked familiar," one of the guys said. They'd all been introduced, but other than Gus, I hadn't managed to hold on to any of their names.

Familiar? There hadn't been a photo with that article, had there? It hadn't even published my name. Had there been some follow-up?

"Cam, wow, I guess I wasn't putting two and two together. I'm so sorry about all this," Colin said, patting my arm.

I sipped my beer. "I tried to call you. This morning. When I realized I'd forgotten dinner."

Now he looked sheepish. "Um. Turned off my phone last night. Beth called. I didn't want to talk to her. Not just then."

"Oh." I glanced helplessly around the table. The men were watching me raptly, as if waiting for me to produce some other amazing trick. I turned back to Colin. "Are you free tonight?"

He gave me a gentle smile. "Sure thing."

"So, back to that body you found." This was Gus, of the "shut up, Gus" comment. "Did you know her?"

I shook my head. "I'm not supposed to talk about it."

Gus traded looks with another man whose name hadn't been part of any insults, so I didn't remember it. "Not even a little? Come on, what did she look like?"

"Dead." It was blunt, but the beer was loosening my tongue, and I thought my only hope was to keep it fairly simple. "How did you know it was a woman?"

Gus smiled, wise as a Buddha. "I didn't. Until you TOLD me."

This elicited a barrage of back-thumping congratulations on his cleverness. Another man spoke up. "How old was she?"

"I have no idea. I didn't see her face."

"What part of her did you see?" My questioner wore a dirty shirt with a stitched name tag over his heart that said "Honda." I didn't know if that was his name or his employer.

I knew I'd better get out of there before I unwittingly blabbed everything to everyone. "I actually can't tell you any more than I have."

He peered at me, deadly serious. "Well, listen…was she…naked?"

"Jeez, Turk!" Gus exploded at him. "What the—"

"That ain't how you talk around a girl!" the fourth fellow cried. "Ain't you got no MANNERS?"

Colin gaped at them and then at me, stricken. "Cam, these guys, I…"

I put my beer down with a thump. "I have to go. I'll see you tonight, Colin."

❧

I left the Lower Tavern nursing a slight buzz from the Heineken, so I decided I'd walk it off, even though the Island Hoppin' Brewery was a bit of a hike from there.

Deliberately not thinking about what had happened the last time I'd decided to go for a walk, I made my way back up Prune Alley, which turned into North Beach after a few blocks, on its way to Mount Baker Road.

Halfway there, my phone rang. I pulled it out of my pocket: Diana Brixton. I swiped to answer. "Hello, Diana."

"Camille! I've just heard the news. What is *happening* up there?"

"Oh, it was very scary, but don't worry, I'm all right—"

"Of course you are," she interrupted. "The body wasn't on *our* property, was it?"

"No, it wasn't—it was a ways down the beach. I was out walking—"

She gave a snorting sigh—somehow both relief and chagrin. "On someone *else's* property?"

"Um, along the beach? Isn't the beach public access?"

"No, it is not. Listen, Camille Tate: it is dangerous to go poking around where you do not belong. I hired you to caretake our property, not to go hunting up dead bodies. Do you understand?"

"Yes, Mrs. Brixton."

"Good." Now her tone softened considerably. "I'm sure it must have been very frightening for you: it has certainly given me a start. The world is a dangerous place, and we would all do well to remember that."

"I…well, Orcas Island hasn't seemed all that dangerous to me…" I faltered. Had it? I didn't know what to believe anymore.

"I fear no place is safe in this world." Another sigh, this one long-suffering. "In any event, it is too late to change our plans: we will still be celebrating Thanksgiving on the island. Please remember to have the house in order for our arrival."

"Yes, of course, Mrs. Brixton."

"Was there anything else?" she asked, as if *I* had called *her*.

"Um, no, that's all."

After she rang off, I shook my head, continuing toward the brewery—my third bar of the day. If I didn't know better, I'd almost think my own employer had been the one to leave the "Mind your own damn business" note.

ↁ

The Island Hoppin' Brewery was not hoppin' in the least when I arrived. And someone else was working behind the bar: a pleasant-looking middle-aged woman. I didn't know if I was disappointed or relieved not to see Brian there. I'd have liked to talk to him a bit more, while I was actually sober.

Because he'd seemed friendly, that was all. Sure, he was cute; but I was looking for *friends*.

At least there were no other customers to recognize me and point and whisper. I quickly bought a growler of Old Madrona, paid, and walked back down into town. Yes, I'd sobered up, but the brilliance of my plan was dimmed somewhat by how heavy the growler felt after carrying it all the way back to my car. I thought it was probably a bad idea to take it into the sheriff's station, so I stashed it in my backseat, then called Kip. Calling was easy, thanks to the number being programmed into my phone. Had I done that? Had he? It bothered me not to know. I stood staring at the CPR dummy hanging in the window while the phone rang, transfixed by the creepy pinkness of the thing. Why was that there? Was it a joke?

"Deputy Rankin." His voice was so smooth, he should have been on radio.

"It's me. Camille Tate. I'm at the station."

"So am I, almost." I turned to see his little SUV pulling into the drive. It seemed redundant to say goodbye, so I just hung up.

That seemed rude, even though Kip was getting out of his car as I did it. "Hello." He smiled a sad little smile. I wondered if all the smiles I'd get here from now on would be rueful.

In no time, Kip had me established in what passed for a comfortable chair, a cup of bad coffee in my hand. I appreciated that he was trying to make me comfortable, but seriously nothing could set me at ease.

"Do you mind if I tape this?"

I shrugged. "It's all the same to me. I just want it over with."

"Can you just tell me what happened in your own words, Ms. Tate."

I took a sip of absolutely terrible coffee and began describing the morning walk with Jen down to the shared dock. "We just walked a short ways—a little ways toward Lisa Cannon's, then back along the bay. Jen had to go back to work, so she went up to the house, where her van was parked."

"And this is Jen Darling?" He was actually making a note.

"Yes. She brought by some zucchini muffins. She made them herself with one of the zucchinis I keep finding on my doorstep. Two dozen, actually."

"She left a dozen here. They're very good."

I nodded vigorously. "They are. I had one this morning."

Kip sighed and looked me in the eye. "As fascinating as all this talk of baked goods is, we do need to get to the matter at hand, Ms. Tate."

And I knew I could stall no longer. I was grateful for the trace of beer in my system as I talked through my walk up the bay, how my mind had been engaged in memories of the past triggered by all the driftwood. I told him about the gallery show, the muse sculptures, all of it. I described as best I could how I'd thought the woman's shape in that tangle was just a piece of wood that had been artfully smoothed and shaped by the water. "I was upset when I saw her, when I recognized that I was looking at a person. So I froze. I do that when I'm afraid, I don't run, I hold still." I was even telling the truth, sort of. "I had to stand there for a minute before I could move. But my phone was back at the house, so I had to move. I walked back and called you, and the rest you saw for yourself."

He nodded. "And did you approach the body, touch it or disturb it in any way?"

"No. When I realized what I was seeing, I couldn't move. I told you that."

"But after you could move?"

I put my arms around myself, an involuntary hug. "No. I didn't go any closer. I just went home and called you."

"And did you recognize the body? Can you tell me who it was?"

I shook my head.

He gestured gently toward the tape recorder. "Can you please say your answer out loud, Ms. Tate?"

I kept shaking my head as I answered. "No, I didn't recognize her. But I didn't see her face, either."

"Not even when she was rolled over?"

"No. I couldn't bring myself to look." I looked into his cool eyes, and felt an unaccountable coolness settle through me. Even the air around me felt cooler. "I wouldn't expect to recognize anyone. I haven't met that many people here. But I think I know who she is."

Kip made a little steeple of his fingers, and looked at me over it with utter calm. "Do you now? I wonder how you could, Ms. Tate. We have no missing persons reports open on Orcas Island. But based on the photo in her passport, we have a tentative identification of the body."

We stared at each other for a full ten seconds. We both knew that there was a person unaccounted for on Orcas Island. A person I'd been asking about since the day after my arrival; a person who had left a note in the fireplace and a passport under a mattress.

I finally spoke. "So it's Megan."

"Tentatively, yes. We're waiting for her parents to arrive for a final ID. The body is at a forensics lab in Bellingham, at least until it's been decided in which waters the death took place…if, indeed, the death took place in the water. There's really no point in speculating until the lab is through with its work." He reached over and turned off the recorder.

"You wouldn't listen to me…"

He held up a hand. "If I couldn't discuss it before, I certainly can't now. You're a person of interest, Ms. Tate. Please be available for more questions, should they arrive. And if you think of any-thing—anything at all besides an accusation—please don't hes-itate to call me, day or night. You have my number." He stood, and so did I, setting my cold cup of coffee on the table. I left without another word.

I wasn't angry. I was furious.

CHAPTER 12

The day went somewhere. Or maybe nowhere. I came home and paced through the house, trying to make sense of what I knew and what I didn't. I argued with no one about Megan, laying out my trail of evidence and demanding that someone, somewhere take notice. I was trying to convince some unseen audience that if Kip Rankin had just *listened*, just taken me *seriously* instead of dismissing me and placating me and doing everything but patting me on the head and saying "there, there," that there might have been a way to *help* Megan.

Maybe even to *save* her.

Lisa was right, absolutely right: we women *did* doubt ourselves, every step of the way. And condescending jerks like *Kip* just added to the problem with their mansplaining and discounting. Why had I let him do that?

Why did I always doubt things I saw with *my own eyes?*

Well, maybe I convinced my defender James, anyway, judging by the twitch of his tail, his fascination with my angry words and dire gesticulations.

Finally, I wrote down everything I knew about Megan Duquesne and emailed it to my brother. I had to tell *someone.* And he wouldn't pull any punches with me. If he thought I was a raving idiot, he'd let me know. And if not? At least one person on this earth would have all the details and see why I was so worried and maybe even be on my side in this thing.

I exhausted myself with all that anger, and collapsed on the bed for a nap.

I woke when it was getting dark again, and realized how late it was. I barely had time to shower and dress myself in something presentable and decide that it was too dressy at the last moment resulting in an emergency attempt to look casual, which is how I came to be wearing my rubber boots with jeans and a silk blouse as I drove down to the West Sound harbor in the suddenly pouring rain, to find Colin's boat.

He'd said it was a thirty-three-foot sloop tied up at berth 14-C. That all seemed pretty straightforward. But by the time I'd found a place to park in the rainy dark, at an unfamiliar marina, I was feeling anything but straightforward. I walked around a bit, but there were way too many piers, and none of them were labeled, at least not so I could see at first. I had to stop and calm myself several times, just so that I would be visible by the time I finally found the darn thing. Small harbor though it was, there were still a *lot* of boats. As one would expect. At a marina.

At last, I knew I'd arrived at the right place. The gorgeous man standing by the hatch, holding a huge umbrella, was my first clue. His looks did their usual dazzling of my senses, resulting in my blurting, "The boat matches your truck. They're both red." The most intelligent and observant thing Woman has ever said to Man since the history of time began, I am sure.

Nevertheless, he smiled. "And your boots. Happy accident, though. Truck and boat are both ancient and well loved. Come aboard. You've had a helluva couple of days."

"You have no idea."

"Oh, I might." He reached a hand up to help me down the few steps into the cabin, then closed the umbrella after giving it a good shake. He stowed it somewhere mysterious, behind the ladder.

Once inside, I took off my raincoat and handed him the growler. "I hope this is okay."

Colin laughed, his eyes crinkling gorgeously at the corners as he took both jug and dripping coat. "If you like it, then it's great. Which one is it?"

"The Old Madrona."

"Works like a charm."

"Whew. I did an over-thorough job of tasting all their options, so my judgment got a little compromised, but I seem to remember liking this one a lot."

"It's a good one." He closed the hatch, blocking out the cold wet weather, then showed me to a place to sit, on a padded bench alongside the wall, pull-down table before me. "First things first," he said, opening the big bottle.

"It smells good in here." I looked around at the tiny, cozy space. It was a combination kitchen/living room/dining room: two-burner stove and sink at one end under the ladder, two built-in benches along the sides, the table taking up most of the middle of the room. At the front of the space was another closed door, leading, I assumed, to his sleeping space.

Colin meanwhile had poured two glasses of beer. The amber-colored liquid rocked gently with the movement of the boat on the water beneath us, as did my stomach. Oops. "Here you go." He handed me a glass, then raised his. "Welcome to my humble home."

"Thank you for having me." We clinked and he sipped. But after my beer adventures of the other night, I wasn't quite ready. Maybe it was the memory of Megan's body, tangled up in all that driftwood. The boat rocked again, and so, once more, did my stomach. I set the glass down without drinking, and thankfully he didn't notice.

"Yep, that'll do," Colin said, then set his glass down on a tiny bit of counter next to the stove. "Dinner's almost ready—just have to put a salad together. You relax there. You've earned it."

"Aye aye, Captain." He was right. I'd earned some relaxation. Maybe tonight would help me put all the craziness aside, at least for a little while. Time with Colin tended to do that.

"I'm sorry about those jerks in the Tavern this morning."

I shrugged. "That's all right. They were just curious."

"Well, they didn't have to be such buttheads about it." He turned his attention to lettuce and vegetables, chopping expertly on a minuscule cutting board. I watched his broad shoulders as he moved easily, comfortably, in the small space. His deft hands, his muscular forearms reminded me of Kevin working diligently over the cutting board in our minuscule Seattle apartment, his careful knifework, holding a spent wooden match in his teeth so the onion wouldn't make him cry.

Stop it, Cam.

I wiped a tear from my eye. I'd never needed someone as much as I did this week, at least not in my adult life. I wanted Kevin. And they didn't seem to be getting any weaker, these longings. It just got worse every day.

"So, feel like talking about it?"

I'm sure I cringed, thinking Colin could read my grief in my face. Then it hit me; Colin wasn't talking about Kevin. He was talking about something much more important. "I would tell you if I could, but I don't want to muck up the investigation."

Colin nodded. "I bet. I hear the FBI's getting involved. Because they don't know where she died. Might have been international waters. I also heard that the body is probably Megan Duquesne."

"Did you know her?"

He shook his head as he began putting dishes and then food on the little table. "I don't think she was here long enough for me to even notice who she was." He topped off the glasses. "All right, here we go!"

I couldn't imagine eating, but I leaned forward, breathing in the aroma wafting from the big serving bowl. Rain pattered on the deck above us. My stomach gave a surprising little flop of hunger. "Wow, what is that?"

"Fish stew," he said, spooning white rice onto my dish—something halfway between a plate and a bowl—then onto his. "I'm sure it's got a fancy name too, but, you know."

I wondered what Kevin would have called it. Zuppa di Pesce? Cioppino? And I felt my throat tighten again. *Cam, let it go. Kevin isn't here to make you feel better, but you have some friends. This friend. Colin is trying, so eat.*

Colin ladled some of the rich stew atop the rice for both of us, sat down, and smiled at me. "Dig in!"

I felt sick from my memories, but I took a bite. It hit my stomach in a very pleasing way.

"Oh, Colin, this is amazing."

He grinned, tasting it himself. "Yeah. Worked out all right, I guess. I get the salmon fresh—a boat comes in a couple times a year, they freeze it right after they catch it, out at sea. Stock up when they come in. Shrimp too."

"This is *so good*. Better than any restaurant. You could make a fortune in Seattle, cooking like this for people."

He shrugged. "No way. Rather just cook for…friends. You ever known a chef? Those guys are crazy. Seriously."

I wasn't going to say a word. I smiled back at him. "You're making me feel very welcome here."

"That's good. That's the plan." He grew a little more serious. "Maybe someday, once you feel welcome enough, you can tell me your secrets."

I covered my sudden discomfort by taking a tiny sip of beer, followed by another bite of the amazing meal. "Secrets?"

He nodded. "Everyone has secrets. Why should you be any different?"

"I told you I couldn't talk about this investigation."

He took a healthy swig of his own beer. "No pressure; just curious. This new thing aside, sometimes you seem so…haunted.

You go away a little bit."

Oh no. I didn't want this to start so soon… Why did it always have to be like this? "I had kind of a rough childhood," I told him.

"Oh? How so?"

Another bite as I stalled for time. "I lost both my parents at a very young age—like, four. I think. It was hard enough that my memories are hazy."

"Sorry." He looked at me, warm brown eyes earnest and caring. "What happened to them?"

"It was a…bad accident." I shivered. "I don't like to talk about it."

"Of course. Sorry." He kept gazing at me. I could see he wanted to know more, and I wished I could tell him, but I was just not ready. Maybe I never would be. When you told people a thing like this, they…got strange pictures in their heads, sometimes.

"Anyway, I had a great foster family. And my foster parents are coming out for Thanksgiving," I told him, brightening my tone with an effort. "I'm supposed to cook for them, and…I'm not sure exactly how you do that."

He smiled. "Do you want some lessons? Or, maybe, someone to come over and help?"

"I couldn't ask you to do something like that!"

"Told you. I only like to cook for friends."

Okay, friends. We were both heartsick, and we were both fine with just being friends, and I needed friends right now. As many as I could find.

The sound of the rain increased dramatically, drumming over-head, sounding almost like footsteps. No, wait, they actually *were* footsteps, I realized, just as I heard a cheerful, even saucy, "Ahoy, Captain! Permission to come aboard?"

Colin's face paled dramatically. "What in the…" He got to his feet and peered up the ladder, though the hatch was closed. "No, no, no." He looked so upset.

"What's going on?"

"Something that should *not* be happening."

"I know you're in there! Open up, I'm drowning out here!" I heard a happy female voice call. "I can see your lights and smell your fish stew! You can't keep ignoring my phone calls!"

He sighed, undogged the hatch, and pushed the door open. Drops of rain filtered in. "Beth. What are you doing here?"

A gorgeous dark-haired woman climbed down into the cabin, then froze as she saw me, her smile falling away. "Oh. I, uh. Oh."

"Yes, that's right, *Oh*," Colin said, sounding cold. "What's up with this? In the *neighborhood*? Just decided to *drop by*?"

She was still staring at me, face blank, a droplet of rain on the tip of her adorable button nose. I could feel my skin start to tingle; I cleared my throat, willing myself to stay present. It would be really, painfully obvious to chameleon away in a cabin this tiny. We were all practically in each other's laps.

"I..." She turned back to him, appeal on her pretty face. "I lost my job, and the apartment...I couldn't keep it, not without a roommate, and I just...oh, Colin! *Already?*"

I cleared my throat again. *Stay here, stay here.*

"This is Camille Tate," he said, stiffly. "Cam, this is Beth Hart. My ex-girlfriend."

"Ex?" She gazed at him with tear-moistened eyes. That was more than rain. "We're just taking a break! I haven't even been gone two months!"

"Beth," he said, firmly. "It's over. You know it. We both do."

"I know no such thing!"

He shook his head. "Maybe you left two months ago, but it's been dead for longer than that."

My frantic mind cast back, trying to remember what he'd told me about her. They'd drifted apart. They were still good friends. It had all sounded so amicable, so reasonable.

So at odds with this astonished, heartbroken woman standing before me.

"Dead? How can you…I never…I went to our house and someone else was *living* in it!" she wailed.

My skin tingled again, harder this time; there was no stopping it. I…vanished. It happens slowly, and then all at once. Silently. I freeze, and everyone else in the room sort of forgets about me. Can't remember me if they try.

Very useful, when you are the smallest person in a dangerous room. Very awkward, once you're an adult with presumably a little more power, a little more strength.

I wished, for the millionth time in my unhappy life, that I had any control over this. Any at all. But with this sudden argument raging, I wondered if it made any difference at all. Would they have even noticed me if I'd stayed visible?

"I couldn't pay that rent all by myself!" he was yelling at her. "What did you think, that suddenly the tourists were gonna start coming in the winter, and they'd want to go out on sailboat rides in the rain, to chase after all the whales that aren't running?" He gave an angry snort and turned away from her, staring at the tiny stove like he didn't remember why he'd cooked such a nice meal.

Because he almost certainly didn't. It's like that when I vanish.

"Colin, honey…" His shoulders sagged, and he turned back to her. "Don't be like this," she choked out, between sobs. "I… need help. I know we…but… I didn't know what else to do." She started full-on weeping now. She even managed to weep beautifully.

The tears worked. He reached out and took her in his arms, and started caressing her upper back, smoothing out her hair, whispering little nonsense things in her ear.

I *had* to get out of here. But they were standing between me and the way out. The way this was going, it was only a matter of time before they would move to the little bedroom cabin…

Ugh, I did not want to see that. I had to make myself visible again, bring myself back into the room. Yes, this was super awkward; no, it was not threatening.

Not threatening. Not threatening.

The first step toward visibility was moving. The fear that triggered the chameleoning made me freeze like a hunted rabbit. But I could move, if I could just talk myself into doing so. I concentrated on my glass of beer. *Move. The. Arm. Move it. Move.*

"Hey now, it's all right," he was crooning at her.

"I missed you," she whimpered.

Move, arm. Move. If I didn't get moving soon, they'd be smooching right in front of me. Or worse.

Apparently, that thought broke the spell. I reached out, gulped down my beer, and set the glass back on the table as hard as I could. Which wasn't very hard, but they did seem to hear it. They each took a small step back; Colin looked confused.

And the beer did its magic. I was present.

I struggled to my feet. I tried to speak, hoping I could make my voice work. Completely inaudible. I looked around and found my purse, cleared my throat again, and made for the door.

Two shocked faces stared back at me. I hated, *hated* this part. It almost sent me back to chameleon again. "Hey. Cam. Wow. You, um, don't have to…hey, don't leave!" He pleaded with both his words and his eyes, looking helpless and confused. *Very* confused.

Beth was sort of frowning at me even while giving him puppy-dog eyes and wiping away tears. She also looked completely confused, and why shouldn't she be? She had forgotten about me entirely for a few minutes. And whatever their current relationship status, he had clearly never mentioned me.

Not that there was anything to mention, really. A hike, a few drinks. Dinner. Nothing at all.

"Call you tomorrow?" he asked.

I still couldn't speak. I brushed past them and clambered up and out of there and got into my car. I drove slowly back toward my lonely little guest cottage where there was nobody but a tiny kitten inside waiting for me on an uninhabited gajillion-dollar estate that I didn't own. The beer and two bites of stew sloshed in my stomach. Tears rolled down my cheeks.

Yes, I was feeling sorry for myself. Who wouldn't? The look on her face, when she saw me in there. And my invisibility had given me a front row seat at a loving reunion. The concern, the comforting caresses, the things they both said… He cared about her, and Beth still loved him, there was no denying that. That was quite a deal on her part, flying out from Omaha, driving to Anacortes and getting a ferry, going to their old house, then to his boat…a long path to follow home, if you weren't sure of your reception there.

But she did it because she loved him.

I was envious and jealous and sick, not because I wanted Colin—but because I wanted Kevin. I wanted Kevin to show up at my door and take me in his arms and promise that it could all be different, that he understood what I was talking about, that he didn't think I was insane, deluded into believing I had some kind of weird superpower, a nutcase…just remembering the things he'd said to me when I tried to be honest made me physically ill.

Well, I was a freak, one way or another. And he was done with me. But the tearful, cooing reunion I'd just witnessed made me ache all over again for what I'd had with Kevin.

I got out of my car, didn't even bother locking it (I was behind a formidable gate and tall fence and it was pouring rain and dark as a witch's armpit, after all), and stumbled through the dark to the cottage's front door. I could really feel that stupid beer.

I unlocked the door and flipped on the light switch, but nothing happened.

"Oh great," I muttered. "Just what I need to make this evening perfect." I stepped into the small living room, trying to remember where I had seen light bulbs. Kitchen? Pantry?

A strong arm caught me around the neck, and a hand pressed a foul-smelling cloth over my nose and mouth. I fought, I struggled, I lost.

That was that.

CHAPTER 13

I woke up in a dark room, lying on a mattress of some kind. Hard, like a futon. An old, sour, flattened futon that hadn't ever been fluffed in the sun. My arms were tied behind me, and a moment of experimentation told me my feet were tied, too.

I guess I didn't come home to an empty house after all.

"Hey!" I tried to yell, but my voice was a rough croak and my throat was very sore, painfully dry. My coughing loosened up something horrible in my lungs. I could taste the knockout drug, strong enough that it made me gag. I spat, aiming for where I thought the floor might be in all this darkness, and tried again. "Hey!"

I tried to sit. I was too weak and far too woozy from whatever had been on that rag to make it upright. I shuddered, remembering the sensation of it covering my face, the smell. If there were ever a moment when I would have wanted to chameleon, it would be that one. But I never went away when I was asleep, and I never disappeared when I was drunk, either. The same rule must apply to being unconscious or drugged.

I lay there, taking stock. I gave rolling around on the mattress a try. Okay, I could do it, but I had no idea how large this mattress was or how far I'd fall to the floor if I managed to roll myself to an edge.

Where was I? *Why* was I?

I kept trying to get a sense of my surroundings, but I could see almost nothing. Either it was a windowless room, or there were blackout shades, or—well, I didn't know why it was so dark. Perhaps that was a crack of light under a door; or maybe my desperate imagination was trying to make it so. I focused on it, willing it to be the light under a door. I couldn't hear anything either. Had the rain stopped?

After a few minutes, the door—yes, it was a door!—opened, and in came Sheila, lugging a big empty paint bucket. She left the door open. Light streamed in. I couldn't tell if it was natural or artificial, but it was strong after the darkness. I still didn't know if I was in a shed or a room. Probably a shed, since she hadn't bothered to gag me. That meant that no one would be close enough to hear me, so I could save my breath and give up the yelling.

I was surprised at how reasonable I felt under the circumstances. How...present. I chalked it up to the lingering drug in my system. "What's going on?" I asked, blinking against the strong light. My voice echoed inside my head like I was in the bottom of a barrel. "Why am I here?"

"Because you're stupid," she said, almost dispassionately.

"This is illegal, you know," I pointed out. "You can't just kidnap people."

She leaned down, frowning. I studied her face. She was a harsh-looking woman, with unwashed mousy hair and pale eyes set too close together; her skin was puckered and oddly shiny. "Looks like I just did."

I shifted a little on the bed. My wrists hurt. "Look. Just untie me and let me go, and I won't tell anyone."

She snorted. "Oh, I believe that. You had your chance to mind your own business, and what did you do? Just kept poking around, and then keep *telling* everyone in the world about it? And lo and behold, you go and find a *body*. What *is* it with you caretakers? Why can't you mind your own *business?*" She shook her head. "Gregory was right, the double-crossing bastard."

My heart sank as I finally understood. I really had seen a murder.

"I promise," I said. "I won't poke around anymore. I'll quit, I won't be a caretaker, I'll just go back to Seattle and never breathe another word of...of any of this."

Sheila peered at me even more closely. "Too late for that, Cam. You can't leave now, even if you want to. And you can't just disappear, either. Not without some help." Despite her harsh words, she still sounded almost dispassionate. Flat affect. "These island cops are stupid, but they're not that stupid. And thanks to you, the Feds are snooping around. I hear Canada's getting in on the action. Canada." Sheila paced to the far corner of the small room. "What a mess. I tried to get you to stop snooping. I warned you. I gave you that damn cat. And you're still hanging around and causing trouble and someone's gonna find you and then it'll be all over for me. So we have to figure out something else, and fast. We're gonna have to do something with you." She fixed me with a hard glare. "Any ideas?"

So I'm supposed to figure this out? "I said, I promise, nothing more out of me!" If I could have motioned *zipping my lip*, I would have. But, you know, tied hands.

She shook her head. "Maybe. Maybe not. We can't risk it. Don't you get it?" She stared at me, something like panic in her face. "You're as dumb as Gregory. Why can't anyone just do what they're supposed to? That jerk. We had a deal. He tried to shake me down." She glared at me. "Can you believe it?"

Um. Okay, so blackmail didn't work with her. "So, listen. Someone will come looking for me."

She hissed her scorn. "Like *who?*"

"I had a date tonight. Or last night. Whenever."

Sheila snorted. "With that boat rat? His girlfriend's back now. He's not going to miss you. No one's going to. Not for a while, anyway."

"My best friend will definitely wonder where I am." Okay, that was a stretch; I liked Jen, but I was just getting to know her. "She drops by like every day."

Sheila glared at me suspiciously. "Your best friend who?"

"Jen Darling."

Sheila snorted. "She's a flake. And I've been watching you; she's visited you maybe three times. Including when the two of you took your little walks. So *stupid*. After I *told* you to mind your own business."

"I didn't, I mean, we didn't mean to find anything...nothing at all."

"Right. But you did. And now this place is crawling with cops. And I'm supposed to figure out what to *do* with you. You're as bad as that cat. I should have drowned you both." She turned to leave the room.

"My mom will look for me," I said, trying to sound convincing. "My mother calls me every day and she'll worry. Or my brother. Yeah, definitely my brother. I play a game with him, on the phone—new moves all the time. Many times a day. If I stop playing, he'll be on the next plane here." I did not add, *From Thailand*. "We're *very* close, me and my brother. We play this game *all the time*."

She stood in the doorway and stared at me, as if assessing the veracity of my claim. Or maybe thinking about how she could kidnap him, too. "I'll get your phone; you can tell me what to do."

My heart sank even further. No way of even sending him a message, in the game's chat function; if the words kept coming, he'd never notice anything amiss.

Heck, his moves were coming so infrequently now, he might not notice anyway. Maybe he would get back to me about Skyping, and notice when I didn't respond? But he was so busy. Probably he'd already forgotten.

Was this actually really my life? Was I going to wake up soon?

"Not so smart now, are you?" She turned to leave once more.

"Sheila?"

She stopped again and looked at me. "*What?*"

"Um…can I have some light, at least?"

A laugh. "In the morning. And use the bucket if you need to. I don't want to clean up after you."

"My hands and feet are tied?"

She cursed, and slammed the door as she left.

⁊

It was a long night. If it was night, and she wasn't just lying to me.

I don't know how long I'd been out with the chloroform, assuming that's what it was, but I developed a raging headache as it wore off. It hurt so much that I was unable to sleep. Or maybe that was being terrified and tied up in a strange, dark place.

So I tossed and turned, uncomfortable to the point of pain; I cried out a few more times, but she never came back, nor sent anyone else in. It all left me plenty of time to think.

I'd spent my life erecting walls between myself and the rest of the world. The normal world, the regular people who didn't have some strange ability to disappear. And now, those walls left me wondering who would miss me enough to notice I'd disappeared for real.

My mother called me once a month, if that. And far too often, I didn't pick up. She was used to it, she tolerated it as she'd tolerated all my odd ways over the years. I loved that about her, how forgiving she was when I simply went to ground. And my foster father? He added things over my mother's shoulder now and then, but never called.

My brother lived in Thailand.

But, I reminded myself, we had Thanksgiving plans. My folks would be here next week. Which was not very helpful right now, but in a week…if I was still around in a week.

I'd been trying to form connections. I had, hadn't I?

Lisa Cannon would miss me. Wouldn't she? She would notice my place looking too quiet, too unoccupied. Then again, my car was there. Maybe she would think I was inside, working on my manuscript. Which she would be too polite to bother me about, till I gave her some scenes.

I was very alone in the world.

I indulged in a spate of feeling very, very sorry for myself. Wishing I was the kind of person who had the kind of life where if I was kidnapped, somebody would notice right away. Within hours—within minutes—at once.

I hadn't even had that kind of life with Kevin, if I was going to be honest with myself. My supernatural disability had forced me to always be evasive, to be protective of my time, my independence. It wasn't safe to get that close to anyone. I'd always had to make that clear, in any relationship: *You cannot expect me to always be there. I will sometimes just need to be alone, no matter what—sometimes very abruptly. And I won't be able to talk about it.* Often, that was enough to render anything a non-starter. Those few who'd made it past that…well, no matter how much I'd warned them, it always came to be too much for them.

Just as well, I supposed. Fewer people to miss me, since I wasn't going to be around much longer, unless I figured something out, and soon.

I had to think. It was hard, my head was still trapped in an aching fog, but thinking my way through this was my only hope.

And it hit me. I was a person of interest. I'd found a dead body.

The *police* would notice I was missing. Kip, he would notice. Even though I'd already answered a ton of questions for him, he would have more.

I shivered—poor Megan. Poor me.

I lay there for another stretch of darkness. My headache subsided, and my mind sharpened. With it came a clear view of my situation.

Sheila could have killed me already. I'd seen her commit one murder almost casually. The fact that she hadn't killed me too gave me some hope. All I had to do was convince her that I'd flee the minute she gave me a chance to. I was good at that, I really had a talent for running away, and I could offer my headlong flight to Orcas as proof of it. *Oh, Sheila, believe me, I'm done here. I'll move off the island altogether—I'll quit and run a million miles from here. You're safe.*

Maybe I could convince her another way. Somehow…

I might have dozed a little bit. Because then I kind of saw morning light, I thought, maybe. And heard noises in the room or rooms outside where I was captive. Voices, an argument, a slammed door. One of the voices was a man's.

Sheila came in, looking actually a little subdued. "You gotta stop shouting," she said. "Someone's gonna figure out you're here."

"I haven't been shouting. I've been asleep," I pointed out, quite reasonably, I thought. "So someone will hear me if I yell?"

"Hush! You're so *stupid!*" She hauled back and smacked me across the face. "Do you want to *die?* Like *Megan?*"

My eyes leaking tears—I hoped they were just tears—I shook my head *No.*

"So shut up!"

Now Sheila sat on the bed beside me and held out my cell phone, as though she had not just slapped me and screamed at me. As though we were friends, or something. Friends who gave each other kittens, and zucchini. "Show me how this game thing works."

I looked at the blank screen, and then at her. "Do I get to talk?"

An exasperated sigh. "Okay, *yes.*"

"You have to turn the phone on. I mean, just that little button at the bottom—wake it up." She pressed the button. "Then swipe."

It took her a few tries, but she got it.

I was dismayed to see that Cliff hadn't played a move. No, this was never going to work.

Maybe it just hadn't registered. The signal was always kind of spotty on the island. And who knew where we were, even. "Push on the little yellow square with the W in it," I said.

Somewhat clumsily, she did. The game loaded up. No one had played any moves.

"Well, maybe he's busy," I said. She looked at me blankly. "I mean, there's nothing for us to do here. He owes me a move."

"Well can't you just send him one anyway?"

It was my turn to look at her blankly. "What do you mean?"

"It's a game. Can't you just, I dunno, play it?"

Was she serious? "Um, it's like Scrabble. Do you know Scrabble?" *Or, for that matter, any other game in the history of game-playing?*

She nodded.

"It's his *turn*. I can't make another move until he goes. The program won't let me."

She sighed and tossed the phone onto the bed. "I thought you told me he sent you a coupla moves a day."

"Well, usually. But never all at once. We go back and forth."

"Whatever."

I coughed. "Can I get some water? I mean, if you're not going to kill me right now?"

"Why do you think I wanna *kill* you?" She looked like she wanted to smack me again. Instead, she shook her head and walked out of the room without another word.

What had gotten into me? Was I seriously sassing the deranged woman who had come into my house and kidnapped me?

But the beginnings of a plan were percolating in my head, and I needed water to clear the drug out of my system.

❧

Once she left, it was quiet again. I finally sat up, moving around a little. In theory, I could stand, even hop over to the unused bucket, but I was not steady enough to manage standing. Not that I could have gotten my jeans down, with my hands tied. Maybe dehydration was a good thing under the circumstances.

I sat, trying to position my ear in the direction of the door, but I still heard nothing.

I tried my bonds again. From what I could feel, my wrists were tied with some kind of cord, looped around several times. It didn't feel like a complicated knot. If I could use my fingers, I could have them off in no time.

I struggled and wriggled, but didn't make any headway on the wrists. My fingers dangled ineffectually behind me, unable to touch anything.

It was dim in the room, but light enough that I could see that I was in a very small, barely furnished bedroom. The room had no mirror, so even if there'd been some decent light, I couldn't have positioned myself to see behind me.

Somewhere in my fumbles, I bumped into my cell phone. Sheila hadn't retrieved it from the bed. "What kind of a stupid kidnapper are you?" I muttered, then said, "Hey, Siri."

The phone bee-booped. "What can I help you with?"

"Call 911."

There was the little answering beep, a pause, then, "I'm sorry, that requires a cell signal or network connection. Can you move to a more open area?"

Well. That would very likely explain why there wasn't a Words with Friends move from Cliff, too.

Maybe Sheila wasn't so stupid after all. Cruel, that was what she was. Cruel.

∽

Miracle of miracles, Sheila came in carrying a plastic bottle. She set it on a tall dresser by the door, then glared at me. I was faint with thirst. "Sheila, please."

She came over with the bottle, then stood there, looking stymied. I had maneuvered myself into a sort of half-sitting position, leaning against the wall behind the futon. "Guess I gotta do this for you."

"You could untie my hands."

"Not even a chance."

She sat down beside me on the futon again and held the bottle to my lips, tipping it gently. She was almost weirdly careful and tender about it. Even so, we managed to spill at least a mouthful or two out the side of my mouth, where it dribbled down onto my shirt.

"Okay, that's all you get," she said, pulling back the bottle. I had to bite my lip to stop from thanking her. As if she'd done me some kind of favor. "You haven't used the bucket, and I don't wanna clean up in here."

"How can I use the bucket if my hands are tied?"

She looked at me suspiciously, as if I were making fun of her. At some point in her tight-eyed stare, she saw my point, but she didn't have an answer for me. She turned on her heel and left, slamming the door behind her.

Maybe she was stupid. Stupid *and* cruel.

❧

Hours passed. Silence outside. I almost jumped out of my skin when my cell phone rang.

I reached for it automatically, going nowhere, of course, as my hands were still tied. It kept ringing. I snaked around on the bed, trying to at least get to where I could reach it, see it.

It was Colin's number. But I couldn't worm-roll to it in time to try and maneuver it into my hands before it stopped ringing.

How did he call me with no cell service?

"Hey Siri."

Be-doop. "What can I help you with?"

"Call back that last number."

Beep. "I'm sorry, that requires a cell signal or network connection. Can you move to a more open area?"

"Siri, the call *just came in*! We have a cell signal!"

"I'm sorry. Can you move to a more open area?"

"No! I'm tied up, idiot!"

"I'm sorry, I—"

"Shut up, Siri."

Siri shut up.

There was no further chime indicating a voicemail. Did that mean the signal had faded again, or that he hadn't left one?

What must he be thinking, after last night? And then my not answering now? Whatever it was, I hoped it involved the idea that I must be in trouble, and that he should send the cops out to look for me, right away.

Yeah, right.

∾

Sheila came back and gave me more water. I sucked down as much as I could before she yanked it away, dribbling a few drops down my chin. What a *waste*.

"There's no cell service here," I said, after trying and failing to catch the drops with my tongue.

"So?"

"So there probably *is* a move from my brother. In the game. But it hasn't reached my phone. I'm sure he's wondering where I am by now. Worried."

She stared at me, trying to find the trick. "I'll take your phone up to the road. There's service there."

Noooo. "You'll have to take me to the road too, or I won't be able to send him one back."

"Not a tiny chance." She bustled about the room, peering into the empty bucket (as if), gathering the water bottle and my phone.

"Do you know how to play the game?"

"I'll ask someone."

I watched her carefully, thinking fast. How far did I dare push her? "I'm pretty good at this, you know. If you put in just any old dumb word, he'll suspect it's not me."

She stared back at me, her eyes narrow and piercing. "You're calling me dumb?"

Yes. I shrugged, as if casual. "No. Just warning you, this isn't going to work."

"What do *you* know." She said it with the tone of, *I know you are but what am I?*

"Does Lisa know I'm here?" I asked.

"Shut up." She glared at me, eyes full of hostility. "You just shut up about Lisa. You don't know *anything*, that's what you know."

"You're right, I don't. What are you up to, anyway?" I asked, kind of astonished at myself, yet feeling increasingly desperate. The longer this went on… "What's so terrible that you need to keep the cops and everyone away? *Did* you kill Gregory? Did you kill *Megan?*"

"I said shut up." She looked like she wanted to slap me again. Luckily, her hands were full. So she just marched out of the room, leaving me alone once more.

She did take the phone. I wasn't sure whether that was a good thing or a bad thing. It wasn't much use to me here, without the use of my hands (and with such spotty service)…but at least I'd known when Colin had called.

Maybe when Sheila showed her smart friend the phone, the friend would realize that someone had called me, and that I hadn't been able to answer. And they would surmise that someone was missing me, looking for me. And then they'd…

That's where my thought process broke down. Because despite what she'd said, if they thought someone was looking for me, what was to stop them from just killing me and dumping my body into the sound?

My skin started to tingle, and for once, I was glad.

And at last, I had my idea.

❧

She didn't return again till after it had been dark for a long time.

My wrists were alternatingly agonizingly painful and numb. The skin was chafed beyond bearing hours ago. I had a gory mental image of it going through to the bone, from all my twisting and pulling, trying to get free. I was trying not to move around so much, but it was almost impossible not to. Maimed by the fidgets, that was me.

Anyway, Sheila came back in and yanked me to my feet, grabbing me under both armpits. "Hey!" I yelled, staggering badly, as my ankles were still tied together. If she hadn't been so solid and strong, I would have toppled us both over.

"Hell." She stopped and dropped me back onto the futon just as abruptly, then whipped out a knife and cut the rope at my ankles.

"Oh…" I sighed, as blood flowed back into my feet, which were now all pins and needles—not from being about to vanish, though I could hardly fathom why not. Maybe I'd used up all my terror hours ago. Maybe this was all just too *confusing* to be terrifying.

"Come on," she snapped, hauling me to my feet once more. "You gotta use that bucket, and then we gotta get outta here."

She unceremoniously shoved me to the corner and yanked down my jeans. I wanted to protest, but the relief at finally getting to go was exquisite. I hardly even minded the audience. Or the lack of paper.

When I stood up, she yanked up my jeans and shoved me back down on the futon.

It was time for my idea.

"Listen, Sheila. I can give you something on me. Something so

awful that once you know it, you'll have exactly what you need
to shut me up."

"Right." She gave me a hard, even look. "Because you're a killer
or something."

I met that gaze and swallowed. "I'm not a killer. I'm a freak."

"A what?" She was scoffing. "I been tailing you for weeks. I just
helped you pee. There's nothing freaky about you, anywhere."

"It's something that doesn't show. It's something…paranor-
mal." I thought about my hours at the public library, the fruitless
search for a word for what I was. I'd been looking since I was a
child, but I never found one. So I made up my own. "I'm a human chameleon."

"A what?" She didn't sound impatient. She sounded curious.
She knelt before me, studying my face. "Look, we don't have
time…"

"Just listen to me." I huddled on the futon, flashing back to
the last time I'd confessed to my deepest, darkest secret. Kevin's
disbelief, then horror, then scorn. The pain of his reaction, the
loss of the life I'd so carefully built with him. But I had to do it.
Telling my secret wouldn't cost me my life. This time, it would
save my life.

I closed my eyes and spilled it out. "I can disappear. I can actually disappear, right before your eyes. I blend in, like a chameleon. I don't know how it works, or why it happens, but I'm
telling the truth. I moved here because…someone found out,
and I want to start over, I don't want anyone to know, and you
do, now. Please don't tell anyone. And I'll keep quiet."

I waited. It was my only gambit, and I'd played it.

"So, show me." I opened my eyes, and met Sheila's gaze. She
wasn't angry. Her eyes shone with anticipation. "I said, show me.
Come on."

I stared back into her small, keen eyes. I saw a middle-aged
woman in men's clothing, a not-particularly-attractive woman,
a not-very-bright woman to whom life had not been kind. A

woman who was hiding out just as much as I was.

It was the strangest thing. I felt no fear. None. My skin was calm.

The one time in my life when I'd actually tried to disappear, and I couldn't.

"Ah, bullcrap." She stood up quickly and grabbed the handle by the bucket. "What a load of *bullcrap*. How stupid do you think I *am*, anyway." Her cheeks flamed with disappointment and shame. She was ashamed for believing me. "You're a freak all right, but you're not a damn chameleon. We have to do something *now*, do you hear me? And you waste our damn time. Damnit."

She slammed the door, but I knew she would return. And she was angry.

Angry enough to get her gun.

I wanted to panic, to erase myself, to pull on my invisibility and go away from this room, her anger, the gun I knew she'd be bringing back with her. She was furious.

But she was angry enough to have made a mistake. A big one. And there was no time to be afraid or pity myself or feel like a failure.

It was time to live.

It was still dark, but I knew where the door was. I kicked my former ankle bonds into the corner, hopefully out of sight, and stumbled to the door. I waited beside it, thinking about Sheila's return, Sheila desperate, Sheila with a gun. Sheila by the dock on my first morning here, the calm way her hand lifted to blow Gregory away on the beach. That was real. A real murder. And I had seen it happen.

My skin tingled and crawled, enveloping me in warm waves of erasure.

For the first time in my life, I was doing it on purpose.

The burning, the crawling, the blanking and nothingness. This was me, going away, this was me, not being here, not being anywhere. Disappearing.

Sheila burst back in, the small gun in her hand raised up toward the ceiling. "Okay, we gotta…" The light from the door poured in over the empty mattress. She stopped, frozen. "I'll be damned," she muttered. "I'll be damned to hell." She spoke in a tone that betrayed her awe, her wonder.

"Unless you're…" She looked suspiciously around the room, her eyes skating right over me. "Damn." She looked back at the mattress and stood there for a moment more, marveling. "You're telling the truth. You really *can* disappear."

Her words broke through my fear-freeze and got me moving out the door, praying I wasn't moving too much air or making any noise. When I started moving, I would soon start to be visible. I had just this much time.

Just this much.

I ran down an unfamiliar and dingy hallway and out an open door—suddenly I was outside. It felt like I hadn't seen the out-of-doors in forever, though I guessed it had only been a day or two. I was woozy, my hands were tied, my feet were still numb from lack of blood and on top of everything else, I was freezing. It was still raining, though not the deluge of earlier. My skin was a riot of crawling, tugging tingles that sparked and itched and pulled. I was terrified enough that I knew I was still completely, totally vanished.

I was also completely lost.

The deep woods were entirely unfamiliar, though in the dark and wet, I probably wouldn't have recognized even the Brixtons' estate. A strong wind whipped through the trees and through my stupid, inadequate clothes, making my teeth chatter. At least I had my rainboots on.

I made myself stop, hold still, pay attention. Through the clacking of my teeth, I could hear other sounds: a car's motor, the crunch of tires on gravel. The lap of water at a shoreline. The luff and crack of a sail whipping around in the breeze. The creak of a boat's mast. I was close to the water. I could almost smell it, even though I still couldn't see it. My attention was almost fully toward the water, though the car's engine was coming closer too. I heard a voice on the boat. I couldn't quite see the water, but I did catch a glimpse of light, and…red? A red boat? *Oh please oh please.* Wishful thinking, I knew, but what else did I have?

Behind me, I heard a whisper.

"I know you're out here. Listen," Sheila hissed into the dark. "Come with me. You don't understand. You gotta come with me or…they're gonna…"

She was completely insane.

My skin was still crawling, since I was more terrified than I'd been, well, except for one night of my life. I wanted to run, but I knew I couldn't. She'd hear me.

I made myself trust in my invisibility. I turned to watch Sheila. The gun was in her hand. She was listening: to the boat, to the sound of the car engine, to the sounds of the woods, trying to hear what was wind and rain, and what was me. Her head whipped around again, back to the water. I was in more danger than ever…but her attention was not on me. She looked like a cornered animal.

I stepped slowly, snaking with my foot to try to find a quiet space to step in the thick trees. I wanted to get deeper, to be safer. If the ground hadn't been so wet, I wouldn't have stood a chance—I'd have crunched the first fallen leaf I touched.

Oh, thank goodness for the Pacific North-Wet.

I heard a car door open and quietly close. Footsteps on gravel. Someone was here, and if he was trying to be stealthy, he was failing miserably. Or she. What if it was Jen? Oh no, what if she got hurt?

I took another step deeper into the trees.

The footsteps on gravel grew closer. I saw a quick flash of light, like someone pulling out a cell phone, then turning it back off.

"Police," called a male voice.

Sheila pointed the gun, her head swiveling in panic. "I've got a gun!" she screamed. "Stay away from me! I'll shoot!"

"You don't want to do that, Sheila," came a familiar voice, from the direction of the water. "Just come on out of there with your hands up. San Juan County Sheriff's Department, here." Kip? Yes, that was Kip's smooth voice, and I might have been angry with him before but I wasn't angry, I was desperate, oh Kip! "Come on now." His smooth voice, so coaxing but firm. "I think you can see that the jig's up, Sheila. It's time to make it easy on yourself."

"So that's it! So it's gonna be me, I'm gonna take the fall?" Sheila kicked at the ground, swinging the pistol in an arc. "Come *get* me, then! Where *are* you? Are you all out there? Come and *get* me! Because she's *gone*, you dirty jerks! She's *gone*, and you're *all* gonna get it!"

A burst of shots, the heavy thud of Sheila hitting the ground, and a burning, searing pain along my left arm—she was shouting, someone was there, two men were shouting—crashes and stomps, people running—my ears ringing.

"Cam?" That was Colin's voice. "Cam, are you here?"

"Where is she? Where is she?" That was Jen. "Cam? Where *are you*?"

I knew where I was. I was coming back to visibility, and the strangest thing was, I watched it happen. I was sort of floating above myself, observing; not literally, but it was like that. First, the pain stopped. All the flicker and crawl, the tingle and burn and pull and ache of my chameleon sensation stopped, overwhelmed by the scorching pain along my left arm. I watched myself fade in and out of visibility as I started to pass out, the strange way I was mottled and patterned, just like the forest floor, almost a part of it. It was almost beautiful.

I was losing consciousness. I knew I would be fully visible. They would find me.

And I wondered if I was dying.

CHAPTER 14

And then I wasn't dead, because surely death would not be this painful. Or cold, and wet. I was shivering, shaking so hard my teeth rattled; and it was bright, torch-bright, I slammed my eyes back shut, they hurt; and oh, so did my left arm, and *everything*.

"It's okay, you're okay," I heard. "Oh, Cam, you're okay, wake up."

I snuck my eyes open again just a crack. It was Colin, rubbing my upper arms. Jen Darling was right behind him, holding a huge flashlight, shining it right into my face, all over me, wildly.

I thought, *I am not alone*. I felt tears squeeze from my eyelids. *My connections*.

"Don't rub her there, Colin, oh no she's *shot*," Jen said, horror in her voice.

Colin drew back, startled, looking at my arm, his hands, the blood, thinning and pinking in the rain. He took off his jacket, wrapped it around me.

I still couldn't talk, but my voice should be coming back soon. Right?

"I did it myself," I croaked in my broken voice. "Me."

Colin took my hand. "Shhh. Stay still, now."

"But I did it."

"Sheila shot you, Cam. Or maybe it was Kip. You didn't do it yourself."

"Not that. The other." I'd been afraid, trapped and terrified, but I hadn't waited for rescue. I'd chameleoned, but I'd done it on purpose. "I did it myself."

"Sh, Cam. Just stay still. Kip's on the radio. I'm calling the fire department," Jen said. Then, a moment later, "Crap."

No service. I wanted to tell her to go up to the road. Wherever that was. Where there were cars, and people. Where all my brother's turns waited in Words with Friends. But not only could I not talk, my brain was going away again.

And gone.

ॐ

I woke up the second time in a less-bright, more comfortable place. Warm and dry, oh yes. My arm still hurt, but less so—a dull, throbbing pain, not the shocky sharpness of before.

"Hey," came a warm voice somewhere near my feet.

My eyes focused. I was lying in a regular bed, a handmade quilt over me; Jen sat in a chair at the foot of the bed, smiling at me. "Welcome back."

"What...?" Oh, thank goodness, I could speak. "Where am I?" I looked around the cozy room. Bookshelves, pottery knick-knacks, a side table with a leggy, sleeping orange kitten curled around a potted fern. James.

Strangest hospital room ever.

"You're at my place." Jen patted my foot, gently, under the covers. "Once the paramedics patched you up, they said you should just rest somewhere. I offered."

"But...?"

"You've had quite a time of it." She shrugged and glanced over at James, who was waking up at the sound of our voices. "There was some talk of airlifting you to America. Your arm was badly grazed by a bullet, but no veins or arteries of note were involved.

You'll be sore for a while, but you don't need surgery. The biggest problem is that you were in shock."

I reached over and touched the bandage on my left triceps. "Ouch."

"Yeah."

"What about Sheila? Is she all right?"

Jen frowned. "That's...the other reason you're here. She was wounded, but she got away while Kip was taking care of you. By the time the fire department got there, she was long gone."

I shivered. "I'm worried about her." It was strange. I was less afraid than I was concerned.

"Don't worry, they'll find her. There's a hunt going on, and her house is staked out. They won't stop until they get her, don't worry. I promise you're safe here."

Someone else was in the room, then. Colin; and Jen was gone. He looked down at me and took hold of my hand. His eyes were so beautiful, that gold-flecked brown. He looked absolutely miserable. "I have to tell you something stupid, Cam."

Something stupid. "Okay."

"It's about Beth. Who left, by the way."

"Ah." I actually had enough blood left to blush, remembering my ringside seat to their reunion. "I, well—oh. She did?"

"She was kinda...panicked. The first time something went wrong in the outside world, she came running back here. Where she felt safe, where everything was familiar. But she doesn't belong here. She'd have been unhappy again in a few weeks, even if I had taken her back. She doesn't really want that. She was just scared."

I thought back to the evening on his boat. How many days ago? Just two? I had heard real tenderness, real affection in his voice—in hers as well. Clearly this was more complex than probably even he realized. She might have left, but I didn't believe they were finished. But that was all right, wasn't it? I understood that completely.

It wasn't as though I had an entirely unfettered heart myself.

I squeezed his hand harder. "It's all right to be scared. That means she's human." I wasn't just talking about Beth. I smiled a secret smile. "So is that the stupid thing?"

It was his turn to blush. "No. It's really stupid. But it made me come out and look for you. I thought maybe you were upset when Beth showed up, and you didn't answer your phone, so I went by the Brixtons' and you weren't there and the cat was hungry. I was afraid, I don't know, maybe the shock of finding Megan's body, or maybe you were upset because, you know, Beth…I was afraid you did something stupid."

"Something *stupid*?" He thought I did myself in because he got back together with Beth? Really? After one drink, one hike and an abandoned attempt at dinner on his boat?

Had I not made myself clear enough, after all this time?

If I weren't wounded, bandaged and drugged, I'd have punched him.

I looked deep into his impossibly beautiful brown eyes and smiled. "Colin, don't flatter yourself. But I'm glad you have a big ego. It brought you out to look for me. Your huge ego saved my life." Well, it wasn't fun to laugh with a flesh wound, but we were both laughing then, and we couldn't stop.

He finally stopped laughing and shook his head. "So, the upshot is, I've…messed everything up. With you."

I shook my head and gave him a smile. "Don't worry. We're still friends."

He blinked. "Friends?"

"Yes. We're friends." I squeezed his hand. "I need friends right now, Colin. Just friends."

He let out a sigh. "Well, all right, then. Friends it is."

Jen entered and came up to the side of the bed, looking down at me. "Let me get you some water. You look pretty wiped out."

"Oh, yes, please." Now that she'd said that, I realized how both thirsty and exhausted I was. She stepped out, and returned a moment later with a tall glass of water. I drank it down gratefully, then leaned back on the soft pillow and closed my eyes.

☙

I didn't even realize I'd fallen asleep till I woke up again. Now it was evening, I thought; golden sunset-light came low through a window over the cat-table. I was alone in the room except for James, who was keeping watch in a decidedly cat-like way. My guard cat. I could hear him purring from here. "Hey kitty," I called out to him. "You're already growing up."

He blinked his round eyes at me, but kept his distance.

I was trying to decide whether to call out or just laze around a little longer when Jen opened the door and poked her head in. "Oh, good, you're awake. Someone wants to see you." She turned and spoke to someone behind her, who then came in.

Of all people, Lisa Cannon came straight to my bedside, warm concern filling her face. "Oh my goodness, Camille! I'm so happy you're all right! Just thinking that you were trapped on *my* property…"

"I…did you find Sheila?"

"It's a tragedy all around," Lisa said, looking very, very sad. "It appears she took her own life."

"She did?" I gaped at her.

"Very likely. The coast patrol tracked her to Crane Island. There was blood at the landing site, and she had left a note. I found it," Lisa whispered, horror darkening her strong features.

"Oh my gosh," I said. "What did it say?"

"She confessed to kidnapping you, though she did not call it that. She apparently had some sort of misguided notion that she was *protecting* you. She promises we won't find her…that it's 'all over'." She shivered, looking closer to her age than I'd ever seen. "She must have taken the boat out to sea—they haven't found it."

I gave an echoing shiver. "Did she kill Megan?"

"I imagine so. She did not say. We'll never know her motive, of course." She closed her eyes momentarily. "When I think of what I did for her, how hard I tried…" She shook her head, then reached out to gently brush a stray hair out of my eyes. "I had thought she was leaving her troubles behind, but some things… I suppose some people can never truly escape themselves."

"You did as much as you could," Jen said, patting Lisa's arm soothingly.

"Oh, wow," I said, my head reeling. I was safe. Was I safe? I felt safe, and drugged. "What was she doing—what was this *protecting me* about? From what?"

Lisa shook her head again. "I couldn't say. She chased a lot of imaginary monsters."

"I thought she liked me. She gave me a cat. Was she just crazy?" I coughed; my throat was raw, still dry.

Jen went to get me a cup of tea as Lisa pulled up a chair on the other side of the bed. She reached a hand out, hesitantly; I took it, and gave it a gentle squeeze. Lisa proceeded to tell me about Sheila's troubled past, her nasty divorce leading to bankruptcy and some subsequent bad choices that landed her in prison for embezzlement. Upon her release, she could no longer find a job. "Potential employers learned about the felony conviction, and that was that. It's a recipe for recidivism; these women have no chance to make a living in an honest way, and it's a tragedy. I met her through one of the boards I sit on. Second Chances, it's called, helping victims of…oh, I can tell you all about that later, it's not important now. I met Sheila while she was helping at an event, and there was something about her focus, the careful way she handled her responsibilities. She was a loyal woman and hard worker, and her life story was horrifying. I wanted to give her one more chance. I offered her a fresh start, new community." Lisa shook her head and sighed. "To think it was all going on somewhere on *my property*. She was clearly more disturbed than I realized."

"But who was Gregory?" I asked, as my mind continued to

clear. "Not one of your actors, after all."

Lisa shook her head. "I thought that's who he was. Gregory is one of the characters in the new play, you see. That's how Sheila explained what you saw to me. And there was no body, of course. But I actually have no idea who the real Gregory was."

"But his boat...?"

"Sheila told me that was her boat, and asked if she could tie it up there for a while. I had plenty of room, I didn't think anything of it. But here's Deputy Rankin. Maybe he could shed some light?"

Kip stood in the doorway with that same relaxed, unhurried stance as the first time I'd met him. He didn't look like someone who'd just finished a manhunt. Womanhunt.

I was so glad to see him. I could have burst into song.

Kip cleared his throat. "We're still investigating, Cam. But this is all part of an active investigation, and unfortunately..."

"...you can't comment on an active investigation, I got it." I shook my head. It still felt cottony, though a little clearer all the time.

Lisa got to her feet. "Well, one thing I do know is that I'm going to be a lot more careful with who I take under my wing in the future. And now I *really* need to find a new personal assistant." She looked at me, tilted that well-cut head of hair, studying my face. "I don't suppose...?"

I wasn't ready to be a triple-jobber just yet.

She seemed to read my mind. Lisa gave a crisp smile and took a step toward the doorway. "Deputy Rankin, do you need me for anything further?"

"They're going over the room right now. It's a process, but it should be done soon. And we'll want to get a statement from you in the next few days," he told her. "But there's no real urgency."

"Then I really should get back," Lisa said.

"Of course."

She left.

Jen glanced at the deputy. "Gosh, Kip, you must be starving. Let me get you some soup or something." She hurried out of the room, but not before I caught a mischievous smile at the corner of her lips. After the door closed behind her, I looked into Kip's cool eyes. "Hello."

"Hello, Ms. Tate," he said, looking down at me. "I guess I owe you an apology. It appears I may have shot you."

"*You* did?"

"It's unclear." Now he frowned briefly. "I know it was dark and wet, but I still should have seen you. When I found you, I thought you were dead." His voice caught with emotion; he cleared his throat to cover it.

"Nope. I'm still here."

He gazed at me with powerful tenderness, relief crossing his features. "And I'm very glad you are."

I looked back at him, feeling my heart melt just a little. "I forgive you, Kip. For maybe shooting me—*and*, for not believing me."

"Cam." He shook his head gently. "I want you to know this: I have always taken your thoughts seriously. I hope you don't think—"

"I know, I know," I interrupted, not wanting to hear it again.

He put his hand on my arm. "No, it's more than that. I must follow established procedures; I must serve the entire public. And that includes keeping *everyone* calm until it's clear there really is something to be upset about. It's not me disbelieving you—it's me continuing to search for evidence, so we can all know what is true and what is not. I've been trying all along to *help* you. Do you understand?"

He looked so earnest. And that did make sense, I supposed; it wouldn't do anyone any good if the cops were always jumping to panicky conclusions. It was his job to be the voice of reason, of skepticism, even. I nodded. "Yeah."

Now he relaxed into a rueful smile. "Good. And I'm sorry, but

I'm afraid I'm going to have to ask you yet more questions. Eventually. But not today."

"I'll be happy to answer anything," I said. *Because you're not going to ask me why I was invisible,* I thought. "But I also just need you to listen to me—really listen to me."

Kip nodded, gazing at me seriously. "Of course, Cam."

I took a deep breath. "So Lisa Cannon thinks that Sheila was insane. And I have to admit, a lot of what she did seemed pretty crazy. But I think she was mixed up in something much bigger. And I really do think she killed a guy—Gregory—that first day I was here. I know you haven't found any body, but I bet there is one."

Kip shook his head, but he was listening.

"And I know Megan was mixed up in this somehow too. If Sheila didn't kill her, then Gregory did."

"Why do you think that?"

"She must have seen something she wasn't supposed to. Ask Jen; she found out something about him online. He was a commercial fisherman—maybe he was involved in drugs or something."

Kip sighed. "Well. Maybe the Feds will have some insights. This is a murky investigation. Perhaps once we have a clear cause of death for Ms. Duquesne, we can stop arguing over who investigates what." He didn't look happy about this. Law enforcement and their precious turf battles.

"But promise me, Kip, that you're going to look for Gregory's body. I know it must be here somewhere."

The door handle rattled without opening. Jen's voice sang out: "Soup's on!" She entered with a tray full of steaming bowls. She set it on my lap, and she and Kip each took one and began to eat. So did I, clumsily, but effectively. I was starving.

Jen looked bemused. "You know, you're in decent shape, for someone who was just drugged, kidnapped and shot."

I looked down at my bowl of soup. I was in far better than

decent shape. I couldn't explain to my friends, yes, friends, I had friends, and having friends was *good*, but I couldn't tell them what it meant to have faced it all down, the fear and the gun and the dark, and lived.

Or could I? Could I be honest someday, tell the truth, maybe even...show them? Could I start now, by telling them who and what I was? I took a deep breath, looked in Kip's eyes, and smiled.

"Chicken noodle is my favorite soup."

Me and my intelligent comments.

CHAPTER 15

Thanksgiving was in two days. Tomorrow, my parents would arrive, and so would the Brixtons. I wondered if they'd all be on the same ferry.

Everything was in order in my little house. Fresh sheets on the guest bed; a fridge full of healthy food and tempting delights, all purchased at the island's hefty prices. I didn't want to think about how much it had all cost. I even had a turkey: a nineteen-pound tom from the Island Market, which Mom had laughingly assured me should be plenty for the three of us. I bustled about the house one more time, checking for dust and spiders, like you do when your folks visit.

Then I headed over to the main house to do the same. It should also be in pretty good order, as I had just been through it a few days ago, but I wanted to be sure everything was fresh and clean, that I hadn't overlooked anything.

Caretaking, yep. Best darn caretaker ever, that was me.

I wasn't completely back to normal, or rather, as close to normal as I could ever hope to get. I still wore a dressing on my left arm to cover the row of stitches the paramedic used to close that path where the bullet tore my skin. I would have a scar, and not just on my arm. I still woke up at night, wincing from the anticipated blow of Sheila's hand when she told me not to speak. I was extremely careful with the alarm system, and grateful for it.

But my sense of well-being was amazingly strong, even after giving my statement at the sheriff's office. It wasn't fun, reliving the entire horrible episode, especially knowing that Sheila had died.

Of course, there were things I couldn't tell the sheriff.

And there were some questions that still hadn't been answered. Our little island was not equipped to do forensic work on Megan Duquesne; her poor body was still on the mainland, being studied for clues. I wondered about the other players in this, Gregory, and how did he really tie in with Sheila? I didn't understand how it all fit together. But that was for Deputy Rankin of the honeyed voice to figure out.

I tried to keep my mind off the parts I couldn't control by focusing on my victories. I'd stayed calm. I'd come up with a plan. My plan had worked. I'd helped myself. Well, my friends had helped me, too. If they hadn't come looking for me, tailed Sheila, hatched a plan, well, I didn't know where I'd be. Maybe at the bottom of the sound. In Massacre Bay. Floating to shore, my hair fanning around me. Like a piece of driftwood.

I shivered a little. But it would pass.

Soon, they'd figure out this whole tangle of a crime; exactly who had done what to who, and why. I'd walked into it like a bear trap, and I was grateful to be out of the snare. But I would be even more grateful when it was all sorted out and put to rest.

I'd had enough of Orcas intrigue.

I stood by an open bedroom window on the second floor of the big house, letting in some fresh island air. The storm had blown through, leaving sun so crisp and brilliant it almost hurt.

Then I heard what sounded like the front gate opening. That was strange; no one had rung the bell. I could hear the crunch of tires on the driveway.

Had I gotten the Brixtons' arrival date wrong?

I leaned out the window in time to see a silver Jaguar park right in front of the door. A tall man climbed out of it, looking as tan and fresh and strong as if he'd just stepped off an expensive sailboat. He gave his well-muscled body a leisurely stretch, popping and cracking tendons and muscles, then ran his fingers through a thick mop of wavy, sandy-blond hair. His eyes were blue, his nose sunburnt, and his *arms*. His expensive shirt strained at the biceps.

He looked up and saw me watching him. He smiled, revealing teeth of blinding white perfection. That smile was like the sunrise, and left me weak in the knees. I knew that face, I'd seen younger versions of it in photos on the Brixtons' family room mantel. He had his mother's smile.

JoJo Brixton.

I smiled back, blushing. I was in trouble. Deep trouble.

Trouble of the very best, very worst kind.

RECIPES

Zucchini-Pecan Muffins
(family recipe)

1½ cups flour
¾ cup sugar
1 teaspoon baking soda
1 teaspoon cinnamon
½ teaspoon salt
½ cup oil (olive or canola)
¼ cup milk
1 teaspoon vanilla
1 egg
1 cup shredded zucchini
¼ cup chopped pecans
¼ cup currants

Preheat oven to 350 degrees. Grease the bottoms only of a muffin pan. Combine the flour, sugar, baking soda, cinnamon, and salt; blend well. Stir in the oil, milk, vanilla, and egg. Fold in zucchini, pecans, and currants. Bake for 25-30 minutes, until muffins are nicely browned and an inserted knife tip comes out clean.

Deviled Eggs
(adapted from *Cook's Illustrated*)

7 large eggs, hard-boiled and cooled
¾ teaspoon grainy mustard
3 tablespoons mayonnaise
1 teaspoon vinegar (apple cider is best, but any vinegar works)

¼ teaspoon Worcestershire sauce
salt and pepper
paprika
Optional, small amounts of any of the following: finely chopped green onion, finely chopped capers, sweet pickle relish, finely chopped roasted red peppers

Peel eggs and slice lengthwise, removing the yolks to a small bowl. Arrange eggs whites on serving platter, discarding the two worst-looking halves. Mash the yolks thoroughly with a fork. Add mustard, mayonnaise, vinegar, Worcestershire, and salt and pepper to taste (note: add more salt than you think; egg whites are bland and require a strong-flavored filling), and mix thoroughly until smooth. Spoon mixture into a small ziploc bag, seal, and cut a small corner off the bottom of the bag to use as an ersatz pastry bag, unless you actually own a pastry bag, in which case use that. Pipe the filling into the whites, stuffing them generously. Sprinkle with paprika and serve as soon as possible.

Baby Bok Choy, What to Do With an Excess Thereof

Wash, and slice in half length-wise. Wash again, now that you can see the grit inside.
Add garlic salt and olive oil to a large pan, and heat. Arrange bok choy cut-side down in the pan. Stir fry a few minutes, until thin ends are limp and thick ends have softened a bit. Serve with scrambled eggs, chicken-apple sausage, frozen dinners, red wine, or a lifetime's worth of regrets and sorrows.

Sneak Preview of
ORCAS INTRUDER
Book 2 of the Chameleon Chronicles

This wasn't what I had in mind.

I'd envisioned a cozy family Thanksgiving on Orcas Island. Something warm and golden, a little fuzzy around the edges. In my vision, I sat happily around the guest house table with my parents, all of us wearing hand-knit sweaters, maybe. We would be drinking spiced cider and laughing over a game of Scrabble while the delicious aroma of roasting turkey drifted in from the kitchen to tantalize us. After I pulled out a knuckle-biting victory, we'd gather around the laptop and Skype with my world-traveling brother.

"My mother was supposed to be here, but they missed the three-forty ferry," I said to JoJo, who had arranged his splendid collection of limbs in the corner of the guesthouse kitchen in order to watch me cook. Or prepare to cook, actually—apparently I was supposed to brine this thing? How do you brine something that's bigger than every pot in your kitchen? "I really have no idea what I'm doing."

"Really." His eyes danced, his expression amused and his tone sardonic. "I'd never have guessed."

"I must be a natural." I peered at the little plastic-y directions that had come with the turkey, dangerously close to calling the 800 number to beg someone on the other line to helicopter in and do this for me.

"You're dripping."

"Ugh. So I am." The directions were covered with turkey water or juice or whatever you called the disgusting liquid surrounding a raw turkey. So much botulism or ptomaine or whatever in that juice, and James was watching me, whiskers twitching, waiting to dart in and get at the drips. "Don't even think about it, James."

He swished his tail and kept watching.

"I have an idea," drawled JoJo, blinking those luminous eyes. I was positive this man had ideas, he absolutely *reeked* of ideas, and the worst part is that he seemed to give *me* ideas. And I was not ready for *any ideas at all*, thank you very much.

JoJo had been tailing me around since he'd arrived the day before. Every time I looked up, there he was, looking rumpled and rich and irresistible. Tinkering with his flawless car when I went to get the mail. Drinking coffee on the back deck when I came over to triple-check that all was well for his parents' arrival.

Even now, as he leaned against the wall by my kitchen window, he looked like he was posing for maximum advantage; his hair lifted by a breeze from the back door, his body positioned in such a way as to show off his broad shoulders, the sun dancing on highlights that were awfully perfect, if they were indeed natural.

It was enough to make me drop the roasting directions. James leapt upon them and carried them right out the back door.

I let out a stream of invective, and then I blushed. "I'm sorry. I was clueless before. Now I'm desperate. And Mom won't be here till like bedtime!"

"Cam, Cam, Cam." JoJo gave his head of gold-kissed curls a little shake and started scrolling on his phone. "We have the internet. Or rather, what passes for internet on this barren rock of an island. Do you remember how much the turkey weighs?"

"Nineteen pounds."

That stopped him. "Nineteen pounds? Why on Earth…"

I gaped back at him. "What? Is that a lot?"

"A lot?" He burst out laughing. "No, not if you're planning on hosting the whole island."

Well, now Mom's chuckle made more sense. "Um, leftovers are good?" If I was blushing before, I was aflame now. "Yeah. Left-over turkey. Sandwiches. You know?"

"Calm down, calm down. I was curious, that's all. You don't strike me as much of a carnivore, to be honest. You have a sort of…" and he appraised me from below his bountiful, tawny lash-es, "…vegetarian air about you."

I stared at the pink mountain of turkey meat on the counter, shuddering at its bumpy skin and strange yellow patches. Hard to believe this was going to be delicious turkey sandwiches in a few days. "I am *not* a vegetarian. But if I said I was, would you cook this for me?"

We were both laughing when a shadow filled the doorframe. Lisa Cannon, looking so little like Lisa Cannon that I almost didn't recognize her. She was trembling, pale, her hair all crazy rather than artfully tousled. Her eyes, blind with terror, darted to mine. "Cam? Oh Cam, I'm…my home, there's…there's been an intruder and…"

JoJo's voice was deep with alarm. "An intruder, Lisa? At your house?"

Lisa stepped in and saw JoJo, then. Her expression of terror melted into actual tears. She ran to his arms. "JoJo! I'm so glad you're here!"

He pulled her close; she trembled in his grasp, I could see it from across the room. Lisa Cannon trembled! I just stared at them both, for a long moment, until he relaxed his grip and she drew back.

"I'll go check it out," he said, manfully.

"Oh, no," she said, blinking away tears and seeming to come into better possession of herself. She even reached up and ran a hand through her wild mess of hair. "It's not safe."

"Did you call Ki—I mean, the cops?" I asked, my hand au-tomatically going to my still-bandaged upper arm, under my sweatshirt. The wound smarted a little less every day. I dreaded getting the stitches out, though that wouldn't be till next week.

Lisa turned to me, wide-eyed. "No. I just ran over here, as soon as I saw..."

"What did you see?" JoJo asked. "Is someone still there?"

"I don't think so." She was calming more each moment, and standing very close to JoJo. Their hands nearly brushed. It looked very...intimate. "But I didn't stay around to find out. They could be."

"We should call 911, then," he said, somehow becoming even taller. He reached into his pocket and pulled out his cell phone.

"No," Lisa and I both said, together.

JoJo gaped at both of us. "Why not?"

I shook my head and looked helplessly at Lisa. She shrugged at me, equally at a loss. Finally, I managed, "There's...been kind of a lot going on around here." My hand went to my upper arm again. At least my skin wasn't prickling; I was *so* not ready to chameleon in front of JoJo Brixton.

He turned to Lisa. "A lot of what, Lisa?" His voice was low, familiar. "It isn't—"

"No—yes—I don't know—Sheila—she caused some trouble," Lisa stammered. "She's gone now."

"Gone?"

"They think she's dead," I managed. "She kidnapped me, and...other stuff. I got shot."

"*Shot?*" JoJo still held his phone, looking ready to punch the buttons at any moment. "My word," he whispered.

"So we've been hoping things would get a little quieter around here," Lisa said, taking a deep breath. She smoothed her hair again. "We've had rather too many authorities around here. I'm sure I just got spooked. It can't be Sheila, back from the dead. It was probably just...one of the actors, looking for something." She gave us both a brave smile. "I'm sorry to give you both a fright."

"Well, I'm going to check it out," JoJo said, shoving his phone back into his pocket.

"I'm going with you," I blurted out. *Why?* I immediately asked myself. Was I a moron? Did I *want* more intrigue in my life? Yet I followed him to the back door.

Lisa grabbed my hand. "I'm coming too."

"Safety in numbers," I said.

We followed him across the lawn, to the path through the trees. Of course JoJo would know about the path between their estates...he and Lisa clearly knew each other well. I glanced around, but saw no sign of my little fuzzy orange package-thief.

When we emerged at Lisa's, I saw that her front door was wide open. She was still holding my hand; now she squeezed it and let go. "Did you leave it that way?" I asked her, as JoJo strode toward the open door.

"I did," she confessed, looking sheepish. "I got home and saw, and just panicked and ran to your place."

JoJo took a step inside, and halted. We stopped behind him on the porch. "My goodness," he said, turning back to us. "That's... quite a mess."

I looked over his shoulder. The house was a shambles. Her exquisite front table was on its side in the entryway, a decorative dish shattered on the floor next to it. Down the steps in the sitting area, I could see more furniture knocked over, dirt and spilled orchids on the carpet, pictures askew on the wall—or knocked down altogether. I couldn't see the kitchen from where I stood, but the number of dishes on the hall floor—broken and whole—implied it was as ransacked as the rest.

"You have to call the police," JoJo said. "This isn't just some little break-and-enter. This is serious vandalism...and probably theft, even."

"Theft," Lisa whispered, suddenly steely and in-control. Her old self. "I need to know what they've taken." She put a firm hand out, grabbing JoJo's phone before he could dial. "Don't. Help me search." She turned back to me. "Thank you, Cam. But

I think JoJo and I can handle this now."

"I…" I stammered, stunned at her abrupt dismissal. "You're sure nobody's here?" *And what would I do if there were?* I asked myself. *Disappear?*

"I'm sure," she said. "My apologies for frightening you, Cam. We'll talk soon." And then she practically pushed me out the door, closing it firmly in front of me.

I stood on her porch a long moment before walking slowly back to the Brixton estate. To my empty house, with its nineteen-pound lump of skin and flesh and bone.

I'd been so relieved this was over. And now, clearly, it was not.

Editor's Afterword to
the Revised Editions of
The Chameleon Chronicles

I still remember a TV commercial for the very first *Star Wars* movie, which included the phrase, "Eleven million dollars spent just for fun!" (Because in 1977, $11 million could fund a blockbuster movie—not just the purchase of a modest house in San Francisco.) The Chameleon Chronicles aren't quite as famous as *Star Wars—yet*—but they too were initially undertaken largely for fun. In 2015, after years of hard work at writing and publishing, dear friends Shannon *L.* Page and Karen *G.* Berry—AKA '*L*aura *G*ayle'—decided to resuscitate the fun they both vaguely remembered finding in their work, once upon a time, by writing something collaborative with no greater or *lesser* goal than creative play together.

Karen and Shannon are both fans of cozy mysteries, and decided that would be a fun genre to try. And since Shannon and her husband (by way of full disclosure, that's me) had been helping to run a B&B on Washington State's Orcas Island during the winters, and fallen in LOVE with the place and its amazing people, she and Karen decided to set their story there. Thus, a sort of literary "play date" project was launched.

And it worked! They had a blast discovering Cam and her strange "gift," fictionalizing Orcas Island, and inventing the weirdly wonderful—or dreadful—people in Cam's old life and her new one, and letting their creativity run wild. Before long, *Orcas Intrigue* was finished, and even had a great cover courtesy of Shannon's in-home captive illustrator (also me), and they were off to book two. That first book sold…let's say *modestly*, at best. But who cared? This project had never been about sales. Book two, *Orcas Intruder*, was even more fun—and had another great cover! Book three, *Orcas Investigation*, was the zaniest installment yet; and its cover had both a *cat* and a *bunny* on it! Who ever gets wins like that back in the serious publishing world? Nobody, that's who.

About that time, their generous and talented volunteer editor needed to step away from his role. So, Shannon brought the *Orcas Investigation* manuscript to her husband, and said, "Hey, honey, we need an editor." (Fortunately, I'm not half bad at that either.) "Would you mind looking this over before we put it up for sale?" Until that moment, I had largely stayed out of the process, beyond cover design. But I happily dove in, and started finding…issues.

They were small issues, for the most part: little continuity errors within or between the three existing books, and a few typos. But there were also a few slightly larger issues that I thought wanted attention. Fortunately, the "Laura Gayles" were happy with my kibitzing, and I'd really enjoyed dipping into their adventure, so we agreed I'd continue as both their cover illustrator and their editor.

By that time, Shannon and I had moved full-time to Orcas Island, and gotten to know the staff at Darvill's—the island's dynamic, well-trafficked independent bookstore—who offered to put some copies of *Orcas Intrigue* and *Orcas Intruder* out for sale. To everyone's surprise, I think, Darvill's kept calling to ask for more copies. To be recklessly candid, we initially suspected they were just being bought by tourists, more as vacation souvenirs than anything else; but we began watching to see how many people, if any, would come back for the subsequent books. To our delight, that turned out to be many more than expected—including a surprising number of locals.

One day I walked into Darvill's to deliver another case of books and hung back when I found the counter staffer in animated conversation with a customer.

"If I pay for it now, and give you her address," said the customer, "could you just ship it whenever it comes in?"

"We could do that," said the counter person.

"Any idea when that might be?" the customer asked, riffling through her purse for a credit card. "She's really been badgering me for it."

The staffer turned to smile at me. "Well, the author's husband is actually standing right behind you. He might know."

The customer turned to face me as if I were Taylor Swift's manager. "Your *wife* writes these?"

"She does," I answered, tickled to discover it was our books they'd been discussing.

"Oh! They're wonderful!" she exclaimed. "My daughter's dying for the next one."

"That's great," I said, eager to tell Shannon about this encounter. "She's hard at work on it. Is your daughter from around here?"

"Oh no," the woman said. "She lives in Arizona. Never even been here."

"Really…" I replied. So…not just a souvenir or "local interest," then. Interesting.

The "L.G.s" were charmed by my tale, but the pandemic had thrown everyone's lives into disarray by then, and it was over a year before I finally got a look at the manuscript for book four, *Orcas Illusion*. Every writer we know has a "pandemic book" story, and this book was no exception. Both Shannon and Karen were struggling with this manuscript, well aware that they had only this and one more book left in their planned five-book arc to tie everything together; and the initial draft of *Orcas Illusion* had bigger character and plot continuity issues than ever. So began several months of intensive and somewhat anxious brainstorming about how to come up with a credible and specific exit strategy to reconcile all the "whimsically spontaneous" ingredients and detours already cemented into the three published books.

Meanwhile, the impact of real passion and enthusiasm on a creative project's quality and eventual success had sort of snuck up on us as well. Karen and Shannon had poured indescribable amounts of love and fun into this project, and as we all worked to get book four more on track, Darvill's was selling through a case or two per month now—of all three books, not just the first one. Clearly not just souvenirs. That December, Shannon and Karen were notified that *Orcas Intrigue* had outsold any other book in Darvill's' entire inventory that year. Sales had even begun to climb online—not enough to make anyone even a little rich, but the writing project Karen and Shannon had launched "for fun" seemed to be attracting an ever-larger audience. Which made all the plot and story arc questions surfacing in *Illusion* even more... urgent.

Well, they muscled through, did a great job of pulling it together, and seemed to be having as much fun as ever doing it. *Orcas Illusion* joined its three sisters in flying off the shelves at Darvill's.

And then it was time to write the series' final volume, *Orcas Intermission*, and tie so many threads into a credible and satisfying bow. For months, Shannon and I talked over coffee every morning about how to reconcile and resolve all the series' elements, large and small. As the L.G.s worked away at that miracle, Darvill's had begun selling a case or two of the first four books almost every *week*, and keeping a list of anxious readers who'd pre-ordered the final book. "When's it coming?" everyone kept asking. "Soon," the L.G.s kept cheerfully replying, trying not to sound nervous. The series had continued to be the bookshop's annual top seller for three years running, and it was time to fulfill the bargain any author makes with her readers—whether their existence had been anticipated or not.

Karen and Shannon did it—pretty magnificently, in my admittedly biased opinion. But not without a few small tweaks to the series' earlier books written in those carefree days gone by. Hence this revised second edition of The Chameleon Chronicles: in which a few loose threads and previously unnoticed typos have been updated to make this whole rather magical tale—both Cam's, and Karen and Shannon's—as perfect as it ought to be.

We *all* hope you enjoy reading them as much as the L.G.s enjoyed writing them.

Mark J. Ferrari
March, 2023
Orcas Island, Washington

ACKNOWLEDGMENTS

This book was a collaboration from day one. The imaginary Laura Gayle wishes to thank the very real authors Shannon Page and Karen G. Berry for inventing her and letting her have such fun penning this tale.

But even two minds were not enough. Shannon and Karen are greatly indebted to the following kind souls: Bogdan and Carol Kulminski, for lovingly running the Blue Heron Bed & Breakfast, a haven of welcome and beauty, for so many years; Sergeant Herb Crowe of the San Juan County Sheriff's Department, for the fascinating ride-along and for answering so many, many questions; and Tina Connolly, for her embodiment of Cam. A special thanks goes out to the members of Book View Café who helped bring this book together, especially Phyllis Irene Radford, Chaz Brenchley, and Vonda N. McIntyre. Heartfelt thanks to Mark J. Ferrari, for the gorgeous, evocative cover.

Any remaining errors or misrepresentations of how the world (and particularly law enforcement) works are all Laura's fault. Shannon and Karen have nothing to do with them.